The Radium Pool

Books by Ed Earl Repp

EMPTY HOLSTERS
SUICIDE RANCH
MUSTANG MESA
HELL ON THE PECOS
GUN HAWK
HELL IN THE SADDLE
DON HURRICANE
CANYON OF THE FORGOTTEN
HELL'S HACIENDA
RIO GRANDE

Ed Earl Repp

THE RADIUM POOL

WILDSIDE PRESS

CONTENTS

The Radium Pool

Introductory Note

To begin with, you may not believe this story, yet I sincerely urge you not to allow the apparent strangeness of it to create a prejudice against it. Many weird tales, most of which are true, come from the vast wastes of desert jungles. How little we actually know of Death Valley—the lowest spot on earth and the hotest! With its shifting sand-dunes, sun-baked hills, saline formations and mysterious atmospheres, the Valley of Death has long been the subject of mysteries for fiction and fact. In truth, it is the one spot on the North American Continent that has not been thoroughly explored either by desert rat or scientist. This is true especially of what lies beneath the surface. Neither has it been thoroughly explored on the surface—the area is too great—and it has never been found possible to remain there for any length of time! Only those who have spent much time in Death Valley can appreciate its intriguing mysteries, its radiant beauty and deathly lure!

I

A Choice Assignment

AT MY LITTLE DESK TUCKED away in the corner of the editorial rooms of the *Outstander*, behind the broad, paper-littered table of the city editor, I sat praying for something to happen. Anything would do that would break the spell of semi-consciousness that had captured me during a lull in city news.

As I dozed, I dreamed of visiting the glacier at Bishop. Then I floated down to Rio de Janeiro. From there, all in a period of perhaps several quiet minutes, I traveled to San Juan Capistrano where I found that the old Bells of San Juan Mission were ringing loudly for the first time in a half century. I awoke with a start. The telephone on the city desk was jangling like a fire-bell.

I sat dazed for an instant. Then my brain cleared from its inertia and I sat back expecting something to happen. I heard the City Editor slam down the receiver. His swivel chair squeaked as he spun around.

"Dowell!" he called, lustily.

"Yes sir!" I answered, rubbing my bleary eyes.

"Oh, I see you snapped out of it, eh? I was figuring to have the janitor bring you a cot to sleep on—or send you to a hotel for a rest, or——"

"Or tell me to take a vacation, huh?" I returned. "This is a helluva day!"

"Where'd yuh like to go, Dowell?" he asked.

"North Pole, boss! Or maybe up to Bishop to sleep in one of those glacial caves they rave so much about. Ought to be cool there."

"That's a good one on you, Dowell. But I am going to give you a little vacation in appreciation of your commendable work of late. I'm mighty sorry I can't let you go to the North Pole or to Bishop either. You're going to Death Valley!"

"I'm what!"

"I said you leave for Death Valley and I don't mean in December either!"

"That's fine——oh well, it might be worse!"

"It could be, but it isn't. I gotta send you out because you seem to be the only reporter on the staff who understands scientific work. You like geology, archaeology, anthropology and so on. You ought to be happy at a chance to work with a real scientist. You dash out to

Southland Institute of Technology and make arrangements
with Professor Bloch to accompany him to Death Valley.
Professor Bloch phoned in—yes, while you were sleepin'
like the original babe in the woods—and invited us to
send a reporter out to cover his reconnaissance of some important human fossils reported found in the Valley. He'll
be gone several days, will pay all expenses and you ought
to learn something. It'll be a feather in your hat if you
bring in a corking scientific yarn for the *Outstander* Syn-
dicate—and don't forget the bonus offered for the best
story of the month."

"But it's quite out of the ordinary to send the star reporter out on a goose chase, boss," I parried, hoping that
he'd change his mind.

"It is, but not when a man like Professor Bloch asks for
the star hand on this journal. You know he has always
suspected that there's more in Death Valley than anybody
ever learned. Who knows—he might make the greatest
discovery ever as regards human development in America!
I'm doing you a favor, Dowell, but you don't seem to appreciate it! I'd go myself if I wasn't tied down to this
desk. Now get the hell out of here and remember that
if a man bites a dog—that's news. And don't try to make
a monkey out of this paper, either!"

"Okay, general! I'll wire you from Barstow on the
way back so you can reserve a room for me down in the
ice house. And thanks for the—er—the vacation!"

"Don't mention it, Dowell!" the City Editor laughed.
"Have a hot time!"

The trip to Death Valley was uneventful. We camped

at what Professor Bloch believed to be the lost Mesquite Springs. The sun had just settled over the edge of the Funerals and the pack animals which we had picked up at Stovepipe Wells were munching barley at the tail of the buckboard when the professor beheld something bobbing about among the sand dunes. The object was too far away to make certain with the naked eye whether it was a man or an animal. Professor Bloch got out his field glasses and discovered that it was a man.

We watched him for several minutes and during that time he fell seven times. He was staggering in circles and appeared to move only because some hidden power forced him to. Presently he fell again and this time he lay still. So Professor Bloch saddled a burro and rode out to get him. I stood up on the tail of the buckboard and watched the silent drama.

Coyotes had followed the stumbling man patiently waiting for him to die. The professor rode to a spot where they were squatted on their hunkers, circled a small area and found his man. He brought him back to the camp, and after we washed the alkali and sand ticks from his eyes we gave him water. When it was safe enough for him to have all the water he wanted, we gave him food, after which he said his name was of no consequence but he had been foreman of the Panamint Mining Company over Balch way. Hysterically he told us that he had lost his partner, interspersing his words with fragments of a tale that made Professor Bloch's strong brows knit together and his eyes flash.

"He's gone—he'll never see this world again!" the man

interrupted when I asked him if it were not too late for us to help his partner.

"Well!" he said, hysterically, "He's found his sweetheart, Allie Lane! We followed the trail together and we found her 'way over in hell across the Manalava plain! You can see it way over there in hell—it's the red streak of table land off to the southeast. For more than forty years, Sands had been driftin' over the deserts searching for her. At last they are together.

The prospector took a long pull at the canteen. Professor Bloch and I squatted in the sand beside our tiny cook fire. The mine foreman pointed with trembling hand, towards the southeast where the vague and sinister outlines of a mountain range loomed mysteriously in the ghostly desert dusk.

"That's a terrible place!" he groaned. "We found a band of heathens there where not even a sidewinder would dare to venture. That flat, above all else in these deserts, is the hottest place this side of hell! And the heathens? Waugh!—"

Professor Bloch sat bolt upright and eyed the prospector whose withered, leather-like visage loomed like a spectre in the glare of the camp-fire. His face glowed with a ghostly tint of greenish phosphorescence—like the radium dobbed face of a glowing watch-dial.

"Pardon my interruption, old man," Professor Bloch said, apologetically. "Did I understand you to say that strange human beings exist on the Manalava Plain?"

"A band of heathens, yes!" replied the prospector with a shudder. "They ain't human, they're frog-faced beasts about seven feet tall, with funny long arms, long legs and big heads! We stumbled on them accidentally and they made us prisoners! God help Driftin' Sands and Allie Lane!"

"Did you escape?" I inquired, rather disdainfully, for I was figuring that the prospector suffered from the heat. I glanced over him. His hands now were steady but his lips trembled a trifle. He shook his head slowly and closed his eyes. I accepted the movement as an attempt to shut out some terrible vision from his sun-scorched brain.

"Yes, young fellow, I got away! But only because I was left for dead! And I come mighty close to passing on, too. I got a family over at Balch, and kids that's been needin' me, otherwise I couldn't have made it here."

"I always suspected that a race of peculiar people existed out this way," Professor Bloch put in. "This account does not startle me in the least. In fact, my associate, Dr. Jorg Jamesson, recovered some strange and almost human remains in this neighborhood that gave rise to startling revelations. Lately our astronomers have noticed peculiar atmospheric conditions over Death Valley that seemed to indicate some tremendous radioactive force emanating from the earth's surface!"

"If I remember right," the prospector commented, "Sands and I met your Dr. Jamesson sometime ago around here. We didn't have time to talk much with him. I believe he showed us some bones that appeared to be human. Let's see! Yes! He showed us a skull—a big skull that was twice as large as mine, with an overdropping forehead, and the face of a frog! Those Manalava heathens had the same kind of froggish faces!"

"Then that evidently proves Dr. Jamesson's contention

that a race of freaks exist or existed here in Death Valley."
Professor Bloch slapped a thigh enthusiastically. Then
turning to me he said: "Dowell, I told your City Editor
that something was going to be found out here to sub-
stantiate Jamesson's assertions."

I nodded. "But what's the story about Driftin' Sands
and Allie Lane?" I inquired of the prospector. It sounded
like a good human interest yarn to me. I did not believe
that it had any significance with Professor Bloch's project
but it would make great feature stuff!

"Yes, yes! Go ahead with your story, old timer, by
all means," the professor said.

"Well," the prospector began, somewhat wildly, "As
I said, that's a terrible place, that Manalava flat, and we
were near the end of our strings when we reached it.

"Our water was gone. We had two good drinks from
a barrel cactus before we reached the edge of the Manalava flats. That rotten stuff didn't help any to quench
our thirst. Near the flats we found a good spring with
dead men's bones strewn around it. A fight had taken place
there once—Indians and whites, and they must have fought
for the water.

"The spring lies in a little box canyon opening out into
the valley. Sands and I could see the sun glistening on
the whitened bones even while we were yet a mile away
from them. Our water was gone and it was safer to continue than to turn back.

"The whites had held the spring and the Indians fought
from behind boulders on the hillsides. By the spring there's

a semi-circle of old prairie schooners with arrowheads sticking in the rotted framework. You can find more arrowheads around the skeletons. There are no drafts there and the bones have lain untouched for years. Even coyotes and buzzards have stayed away from the Manalava Plain! I don't understand why Indians, with their superstition, would venture near the earthly hell.

"The spring was worth fighting for, I said to myself, as I ducked my head in the water. The water was cool and tasted good, but it had a greenish tint—that was the color peculiar to the heathens under the Manalava Plain! We camped at the spring all night.

"Sands did not sleep well that night. He seemed to be high-strung and excited in the morning. He claimed that he heard voices throughout the night and after breakfast he began talking about Allie Lane.

"You've heard the tale about Allie Lane, of course. Everybody who has lived in California long must have heard about it. She was Sand's sweetheart back in Kansas City when he was a youngster. He came to California first and Allie, with her father, started West with a wagon train the following spring in 1880. If that train had ever arrived, Sands would have known it. For over forty years he had been searching for news of Allie up and down the coast until it cracked his mind some.

"Allie must have meant a lot to him, for he never married and for forty years he's been drifting over California asking folks if they'd ever met up with anybody by the name of Lane from Kansas City.

"Allie Lane had been a member of a train such as lay

scattered around the spring. This was worrying him, I could see. He was a bit off on the subject after having searched for her so long. It taxed his brain, and Sands was an old man. I watched him as he puttered and poked around those whitened, petrified bones.

"There was a wagon train—the remains of one that had probably taken the southern route across from El Paso, heading into California over the old Fremont Trail. It wasn't necessary for them to head into Death Valley; so they must have gone off the right trail and strayed through an unknown pass into the Valley where they died fighting the Apaches at this water hole.

"I tried to argue the old fellow out of the idea that Allie Lane had been killed, telling him that she had arrived safe, married, and forgotten all about him. But he would have none of it and flew into a rage, saying that she promised to wait for him and that he'd meet her alive in California. I let it go at that.

"I sat down on the wreck of one of the schooners and watched him putter around the bones. He had loved this Allie Lane in the days of his youth when he left her back in Kansas City. I suppose he had an indelible picture of her as she was when he left her, stamped in his brain, and did not figure that now she would be an old lady, even if she was alive.

"So Driftin' Sands continued his two great searches. One was for Allie Lane, first and always, and the other was for gold of which he had found plenty.

"I'm sure that Sands and I were the first to enter that Canyon since the fight by the spring. There was not a speck of ashes to prove that anyone else had ever camped there.

"The canyon was free from sand storms, and sheltered on practically all sides except for the Valley opening; and even if the sight of human bones would drive one away, there was always the spring to lure a man back. But it was hard on the nerves to stay there. There was something eerie and ghostly about the whole section of desert that was not caused by a few bones scattered around. We were to learn what it was later.

"Sands found an old trunk half buried in the sand. It was rotted and sprung by sun and weather and it crumbled at the touch of a hand. In that trunk Sands found an old family picture album. The photographs were so dim that very few were distinguishable. He pored over them nervously and when he had gone almost to the last page, his shaking fingers held a leaf. He found a picture that glued his eyes to the rotted book and then I had my first sight of Allie Lane!

II

What Sands Heard

THE FACE ON THE TINTYPE displayed the features of the most beautiful girl I have ever seen! Her features were clear-cut, her eyes soft and appealing. In spite of the years, that one picture, out of a hundred old tintypes, remained clear and distinct. Underneath the picture was a written description that we could not read with the naked eye. The ink had long since disappeared, leaving only faint traces of point imprints. I got out my magnifying glass that I used to study ore specimens, and read the words:

Allie Lane,
Kansas City, Missouri.
March 19, 1878

"I handed the glass to Sands and went over to douse
my head in the spring. You see, I'd heard the name of
Allie Lane so many times that when I came face to face
with·that picture of her, it fairly upset me.

"Presently Sands returned my glass and without speaking we packed our outfit, rolled in the spring, and struck
off toward the Manalava Plain.

"That night was like all the rest. We wrapped ourselves
in blankets and slept. But toward morning Sands awakened
me.

" 'Pardner! Get up!' he said. 'I hear a wagon passing
off there in the valley and if we hit the trail now we can
hook up with it until we reach the Manalava Springs. It's
a long hike to the flats and water's scarce! Hear the wagon
crashin' through the brush?'

"I raised on my elbow and listened. There was not a
sound to be heard. I looked at Sands queerly. Was the
heat and the excitement of seeing Allie's picture, affecting
his mind, and anyway, why should a wagon of all things
be trekking through the desert during the dead of night?
Anyone but an utter fool would use an auto. But I yielded
to his excitement and we started out at once, leaving behind
an extra blanket and some canned goods so as to travel
lighter. I allowed Sands to lead where he thought the
sounds came from.

"We went on and on, I all the while arguing that I

could hear nothing while Sands insisted he heard the wagon continually.

"Little by little the gray and orange of approaching dawn began to steal over the valley. The world was assuming a definite shape and the day's heat began to mount even before the first rays of the rising sun were visible. A mile in front of us a great, red streak rose against the skyline, looming dimly and awesomely out of the lightening eastern heavens. Sands remarked at its ghostliness and informed me that we were nearing the southern extremities of the terrible Manalava Plain. I had never been in the section of Death Valley and of a certainty, Sands had never been nearer than he was then.

"In some forgotten day a volcano had scattered its red hot lava and settled it into a stretch of plain which covered an area of thirty miles either way, although no trace of a volcanic mountain was visible. Bare and flat as a table-top and as hot under the glare of the sun as the inside of an oven! Such was the Manalava Plain, never explored, unmapped——a lost world of its own.

"Sands kept on insisting we were coming nearer to the sounds.

"Rapidly it became light enough for us to see the Plain. The sun, a huge fiery ball, popped up almost suddenly from behind the Manalava Plain and instantly the world was sweltering. Its golden glow reflected on the red lava of the Plain and created a murky green haze that added to the heat and burned acridly through the lungs. The odor was ungodly and unworldly!

" 'There's the wagon!' Sands suddenly exclaimed.

"I looked all over the desert, and not a thing like a wagon did I see.

" 'I don't see a thing,' I told him soberly.

" 'You don't,' he exclaimed incredulously. 'Why look out there.' He pointed toward the base of a low hill. There was not a thing to be seen. I knew then that his mind was slipping under the terrific strain. I tried to argue with him. I even shot off my pistol to show him that there would be no response. But Sands insisted on going on. Rather than have him travel into that hell alone, I shook my head and followed after him.

"We climbed the buttress of a low hill and swung to the left, discovering a natural causeway that led up and out into the very table-top of the Manalava Plain itself.

"Before us in unbroken desolation lay the forgotten country—Manalava Plain! The formation of the floor was a soft lava-like surface—rock that had once flowed in liquid form and after hardening to some extent, gave the country a flat and shiny appearance like a great field of red asphalt.

" 'The wagon is gone,' Sands exclaimed suddenly.

" 'That's mighty peculiar, Driftin',' I said, 'That they're gone when you said that they weren't more than a mile ahead of us.'

" 'I don't savvy it at all,' he replied. 'But let's follow further. They'll sure need help.'

"Helplessly I followed.

"Here was the Manalava Plain—as flat and smooth as a plate of glass—and stretching for miles either way, bare and deserted. Surely we were the only actual beings on the mesa!

"Perhaps, I thought, old Driftin' Sands was suffering from hallucinations. Perhaps the sight of the bleached bones back at the spring had gotten into his blood. I wanted to give up the chase but Sands declared again he would con- tinue alone. I had no alternative but to accompany him. To me death beckoned either way and I'd been with Sands so long now that a few more miles would not matter.

"Presently we came upon a weird sort of a cactus tree— a species of a kind that I'd never seen on the desert! It was red instead of green and had long, flowing branches like the tentacles of an octopus! The tentacles twitched rest- lessly although there was not a breath of wind to stir them. I warned Sands to stay a safe distance away from it. The thing seemed alive! Farther off, standing dimly in the green murky haze, I saw other trees like the one in front of us. They stood motionless and stiff.

"By all the laws of nature, the trees in front of us should not have been growing there—should not have been on this world at all! We stopped and looked at each other.

"We looked at the cactus closely. Its tentacles were waving spasmodically as though warning us to return from whence we came. I tore my eyes from it and studied the earth. Sands gasped when I pointed out to him the frag- ments of a human skull and other anatomical portions of the human frame, apparently crushed, strewn under the waving, rubber-like tentacles of this weird cactus.

"I felt an urge to dash away from the spot and it was

with a mighty effort that I controlled an insanity that was creeping through my brain.

" 'Do you admit there's no wagon here,' I yelled at Sands.

" 'I guess there isn't pardner," he acknowledged, down-cast. His shoulders seemed to droop more than ever and the alertness in his eyes suddenly disappeared. 'But how do you account for my hearin' a man, a woman and a wagon? They've got to be here; so let's follow them out.'

"My insane desire to run now manifested itself into a reality, and with Sands at my heels, I started off at a run. Eventually I steadied my racked brain and slowed the pace. Sands came up, breathing heavily at the exertion. I noticed that he had cast his pack away and clung only to a gallon canteen in which I could hear the water sloshing around. The sound told me that it was almost empty.

"Presently we discovered the remains of an old schooner. It was just like those back at the spring. Its canvas tar-paulin, bleached white, clung from the top-ribs in streamers of gossamer. Not a single bone could be found in front of the wagon, lending more mystery to the trail. Where had the horses gone? What had become of them? Surely, there would be bleached skeletons in the traces had the horses been deserted.

" 'The horses laid down here.' Sands was saying as to himself, kicking a foot at two wallows in front of the wagon. 'But they must've got up and wandered away after restin'. See, the traces have been cut! The man picked up the woman and packed her off. His trail is deeper now. We ought to find 'em soon.'

"I said nothing. Perhaps he had seen something and I was the one who was mad. Some story was plainly written on this wagon. Sands pointed at the side board. Cut deep were the even letters of Alfred Forsythe Lane, Allie's father. Below the name was a scratched message. With difficulty we read it.

" 'God have mercy on us. Our water is gone—this is the end. I love you, Robert Sands of Kansas City. If you ever see this, you will know!"

"Sands sat down on the rotting tongue of the wagon and cried. His great, booming voice quivered with emotion as his body twitched with sobs. Tears rolled down his withered, weatherbeaten face in spite of the terrific heat of the Plain that sucked the moisture from our bodies. Hands, gnarled with years of toil and sorrow, fondly held the old tintype taken from the faded album found at the spring.

"Sands straightened. His eyes, now dry and dim, surveyed me for a moment.

" 'You'd better take this water, pardner,' he said, 'and hit the back trail! I'm going to follow this to the end and there'll be no return. You take it and go back to your wife and kids! They'll be needin' you, pard, like Allie needed me. Take it!'

"Instinctively I reached out for his proffered canteen. Then I thought better of it. I certainly did want to go back. What would my wife and kids do if I failed to return! But if I deserted Sands I would never be able to live it down. I decided to stick it out. A few more miles could not matter now and the chances of me finding my way out were mighty slender, anyway.

" 'I couldn't take it, Sands,' I said. 'I'd rather go ahead and see what's beyond. I—I—er—er rather like this hike, you know.'

"And so I followed him again.

" 'There they go, pardner!' he shouted finally. 'Down the draw! Hurry and we'll catch up with them!'

"I looked up in time to see two forms crawling on hands and knees down the draw. I was certain that my own mind was giving way to hallucinations, but to satisfy Sands I started forward at a trot. Sands was at my side. As he ran, his jaws were beating a loud tattoo. My heart ached for him and his sweetheart whom he'd search for so long—Allie Lane! Maybe he would find her, I thought.

"Presently we arrived at what we thought was the draw down which the two crawling figures had vanished. Instead of finding what we expected we actually encountered a saucer-like crater which I assumed at once to have been the one from which the lava forming the Manalava Plain had erupted. We stood on the brink of the yawning pit and noted that in the center, surrounded by overhanging lava forming a circular cave, brilliant with a green phosphorescent glow, was a pool probably a hundred feet in width. The pool seemed as alive as that grotesque cactus with its restless tentacles.

"The pale green that filled it, with its ghostly hue, reminded us of the spring at which we found the Lane album. The material shimmered and scintillated and even from our height we felt a terriffic heat that must have come from the stuff. There was a powerful odor coming from it, too, sweet and nauseating. The glare from the pool seemed to burn our skin even at the distance we stood from it. Nowhere was there a sign of the mysterious crawling figures—the man and the woman, although under our feet were the marks of a ragged trail.

" 'Good Lord, Sands!' I cried, 'that stuff could be radium!'

"Sands looked at me with a puzzled frown.

" 'Hell!' he expostulated, 'there's not that much radium in the whole world and we wouldn't know it if we seen a lake of it. Looks like some green salt solution to me and indications point to some funny deposits here! What's that unearthly noise?'

"I cupped my hands behind my ears to catch the sound that Sands had heard. My hair literally stood on ends. Spooky? Lord! I couldn't have moved a foot if I wanted to. I was glued to the spot. The weird sound, like the low moan of a woman in mortal agony, issued from the circular cave surrounding the luminous pool. It grew louder until the Manalava Plain groaned under the tumult. The sounds penetrated to the core of the brain and seemed to beckon us down into the crater. Sands was swaying to and fro as he stood on the slight parapet overlooking the crater, in perfect rhythm to the tempo of the devilish sounds. I felt that I too was keeping the same accompaniment and it was with an effort that I broke the spell.

"My hand dropped to my gun butt. I tore it out of its holster and fired rapidly, thumbing the hammer, into the pool. Sands yelled. Like a living fountain, long columns of luminous green and red and violet flame shot up to the parapet. Simultaneously we both leaped back. The air seemed alive with some mysterious vibrations. Finally it died away and the tumult issuing from the circular cave settled down to a low, steady hum. We once again stood on the crater's escarpment and looked within. The pool was glittering restlessly.

" 'We might as well have a close look at that pool, pardner," Sands reminded me as I stood rooted on the edge of the crater, studying the formation surrounding the pool. 'I can't make it out. If it's some radium compound, you'll be a rich man. Your wife an' kids back in Balch will be needin' it, I'm thinkin'. Let's go down.'

"Sands stepped over the escarpment. I followed him down into the crater. We paused about twenty feet from the edge of the pool. The heat was terrific—so great that it caused the blood to race to my head, and my heart to beat rapidly. And more intense became that mysterious vibration in the air, and a something that seemed to be eating into my flesh. I remarked about the phenomenon to Sands and told him that it must have been caused by some unknown power of radium. Rather than risk touching the stuff I threw a piece of cloth on it. There was a little sizzle and the cloth seemed literally to vanish before our eyes! He then took his revolver and dipped it in. The hard steel of the barrel melted like lead in a blast furnace, yet the butt in his hand did not heat beyond sun-temperature. The melted steel floated to the surface like slag and drifted out into the center of the pool, to sink again in a tiny whirl. Sands fondled his useless gun speculatively.

" 'Pardner,' he said, 'You're lookin' into a pool of some

radium compound! It must be radium for I've seen about everything else in its line. If Allie and her father came too close to this, you can imagine what happened to them. I fear the worst.'

" 'Well,' I said, 'I don't like to think that your friends ended near the pool. We might see some bones if they did. Let's take a look under these overhanging shelves. The caves might tell us something.'

" 'I don't reckon we'll find anything, pardner,' Sands returned, sick at heart and utterly dejected.

" 'Can't tell! We've seen so many strange things that I'm interested,' I said.

"By all the laws of human nature and its greed for the precious, Sands and I should have danced around the radium pool with glee over our discovery. Untold wealth lay exposed before us, but under the sadness of our circumstances, the living, pulsating pool was nothing. The radium, which we believed oozed out of the old volcanic crater, could ruin the world, with its great power and radio-active qualities.

III

Eldorado

At any rate, we picked our way carefully, shielding our faces, remaining as close to the cave wall as possible, peeping intently into the greenly illuminated circular cavern. Glowing stalactites hung from the cave ceilings in mystic forms. Precious stones and metals in countless numbers cropped out of the lava-like formations. Rock which Sands had accepted previously as cinnabar was red rock-lava bearing iron pyrites and black quartz, containing a wealth of sapphire and diamond-like stones that glittered invitingly under the glare of the green rays cast off by the pool.

" 'My God, Sands!' I shouted eagerly, forgetting momentarily my sorrows and sympathies for Sands and his sweetheart of long ago. 'We've struck it! This is the real El Dorado! It is like the myths handed down by the Spaniards! Wealth! Riches! Power and—'

" '—and unhappiness, greed and all the rest!' Sands added, staring at me curiously. 'It means the fulfillment of your dreams, pardner. You know what it means to me? To me it means the loss of all that I've ever held dear in this life. It means that I've spent my life in quest of happiness—and lost it right here at this pool! Do you realize that, pardner?'

"I most certainly did realize it and I calmed down to once again share Sands' great sorrow. He had trailed Allie Lane and her father over the forty-year old trail. Here we believed that it ended forever. No need to search farther. Yet for some unaccountable reason, Sands insisted that she was still alive or if not alive, some remains must exist in that vicinity.

"As we continued our search and explorations near the mouth of the cave, the weird, ominous moaning that vaguely portended the advent of something untoward, became audible again. Sands and I stopped in our tracks to listen. Coming from the far side of the pool, the moaning increased gradually until it became a steady wail like the shriek of high-speed machinery. We stood watching the spot which unlike the part of the crater on our side, did not glow with the green luminosity. It seemed to be an inky black pit. Not even a stalactite was visible!

"Suddenly as we stared at the spot, the blackness became

shot with myraids of colors until it glittered blindingly. The wail was now a terrific shriek. The Manalava Plain seemed to groan under some tremendous impulse emanating from below our feet. The earth swayed and rumbled. From the pool, came a mysterious sputtering and a tiny swirl in its center at first, suddenly became a whirling maelstrom. A thin, silver-like column rose several feet into the air from its middle. Like a miniature water-spout, typical of typhoon infested sections of the South Seas, the rising column whirled faster and faster.

"Meanwhile, the once black, bottomless abyss which had suddenly become charged with blinding colors, was changing now to a more solid hue. Green was transplanting the reds and vermilions, and thin, wisp-like rays of yellow that seemed to charge the atmosphere with a super high-tension activity, were twitching nervously in the pit. Gradually the colors merged into a solid mass of luminous green and out of it spun a glistening sphere that appeared to be a ball of the same liquid that was now whirling over the pool!

"The sphere, probably twenty feet in diameter, moved slowly at first, toward the pool, its surface glowing as it revolved with a terrific speed. The atmosphere became stagnant and penetrated deep into the lungs, but Sands and I were too stupefied to move a muscle. I felt a sudden panic seize me and then breaking the grip of stupefaction I ran like a mad man along the edge of the whirling maelstrom. I was struck with fright. You cannot conceive my terror as I stumbled along the pool! I forgot about Sands—

forgot about everything in my blind unreasoning. I felt no fatigue as I ran, only stark, mad terror.

"In my wild terrified scramble for safety, I ran past the only exit or entrance down into the crater and soon found myself face to face with the spinning sphere! Bright, swift moving lights passed around the sphere as it emerged from the abyss. The yellow rays were gone now and as I stared at it in my utter terror, the sphere began to glow like a great emerald ball. The high-pitched scream was more terrific here and it pounded in my eardrums with a metal-edged sharpness that sent me blind and unreasoning back around the other side of the pool! In my terror I thumped into Sands, who was standing in the same spot where he had been when I started my mad dash. The collision brought us both to the crater floor, clutching for the slightest handhold to prevent us from rolling into the ghastly pool. At the very edge of the pool we came to a stop. Sands put out a hand to brace himself but the tips of his fingers accidentally dipped into the liquid. He jerked back his hand with a bellow. The first digits of his left hand had disappeared, leaving instead, completely healed stumps! The shock of the collision restored my sanity and I helped Sands to his feet.

"We cast quick glances at the sphere. It had moved from the opening of the pit, now lighted brilliantly red, and was whirling at the top of the column in the center of the pool! Gradually the high-pitched scream became a steady hum. The sphere was spinning faster and faster under the whirling pressure of the column. The ball was changing slowly into cylindrical shape, with a sharp-pointed nose and concave butt which gradually thinned out. I stared with unbelief. Surely my brain was playing pranks. I shot a glance at Sands. The old fellow seemed like a statue, immobile as a rock. Insanity was gripping him, I could see, and I screamed.

"Suddenly, the hum of the sphere's rapid whirling motion ceased. Like a bullet shaped projectile it shot into the air, charging it with sparks of pale green lights that drifted back into the pool and settled. We caught a glimpse of the projectile as it leaped from the column. That was all. Immediately it was gone leaving behind only the floating green lights that, even in the radiance of midday, shone brilliantly. The fearful scream of its passing through the atmosphere gradually died away as its distance increased. At my scream Sands had regained control of himself. He placed a palsied hand on my shoulder and stared at me incredulously.

"Did you see it, pardner?" he asked, completely unnerved.

" 'Yes!' I answered, 'I've seen it whatever the thing was!'

"Sands stared at me, mouth agape.

" 'Pardner,' he said, 'you look like a ghost! Your face and hands are turning green! Your skin is getting the same color as the stuff in the pool!'

" 'You don't look like a white man yourself, Sands,' I managed to jest at him, trying to control my agitation.

" 'Maybe,' he returned, somewhat calmed, 'but, by jingle, I'm beginning to feel younger! Maybe this is that fountain of youth the old spics raved about!'

" 'You must have just come into your second childhood,' I smiled back at him, weakly. He managed to grin and I saw something that startled me almost as much as did the luminous sphere.

"Sands' face was actually clearing! Deep furrowed wrinkles that had marked him as an old man, sun-hardened and leathery, were vanishing from his face! Except for a month's growth of beard, he appeared to have dropped, in those few minutes, many years of his age. His brown eyes that were dim, and watery, were taking on a sparkle that signifies the vigorous health of youth. His bowed shoulders straightened. In spite of the rapid change he was going through, the greenish hue remained to mar his features with a ghastly pallor caused, no doubt, by the radio-active power of the radium. As for myself, I could feel no change in my physical being. I wondered if the great radium deposit was to blame. I knew that science held transmutation of elements possible and has even accomplished it in a small way and that radium itself is the product of disintegration of uranium and ionium.

"For some reason, Sands and I felt better after the hurtling projectile had lifted from the whirling pool and passed into the infinite. After a short conference we decided to investigate the strange phenomenon we had witnessed, and at the same time continue our search for Allie Lane and her father, or whatever traces of them might remain. Our brains were clear as bells now, our wits sharp in spite of so many strange happenings that occurred since early that morning. After it all, we thought, we could not be surprised at anything that might arise in the future, and we might as well explore further, the weird circular cave and the black hole which we noticed still retained its red glow. Sands remarked that if the red glow continued to illuminate the cave from which had come the whirling sphere, there would be no need of the small carbide lamp I had in my pack still strapped to my shoulders. The only thing that seemed to worry us was the absence of water. Our canteens were practically empty and naturally we wanted to refill them if we could. We seemed to have no thirst and a strange comfort appeased the dryness of our throats.

"We single-filed along the edge of the pool toward the luminous red cave. In several minutes we had reached the entrance to our glowing objective. At the entrance of the cave with its glow of red radiancy, Sands and I paused before entering. What we saw there caused Sands to leap backward. I stood stock still, awed at the sight, not knowing what to do.

"On either side of the cave, hung intact were the skeletons of two human beings! With skulls grinning like green ghosts, the skeletons hung against the side butts of the cave's entrance! Weirdly radiant with the pale green hue, the bones stood out in high relief against the red glow of the strange illumination as though to warn us that to go further meant doom.

"I turned at the sound of Sands' getting to his feet. He stood at my side, mouth agape.

" 'That, pardner,' he said, softly, 'means the end of our search! I have hoped for the best for Allie and her dad, but what we see now tells the story of their deaths!'

"Sands doffed his hat and hung his head in reverence. I did likewise for I was thinking along the same lines. Sadly I lifted my head and again speculated on the skeletons. I was trying to figure who might have hung those grisly relics on the wall of the cavern. Whoever it was, I thought, had scant respect for the dead! The two could at least have been given decent burials. I clenched my fists and swore. Sands lifted his head suddenly at the oaths which escaped my lips. His hand grasped my sleeve.

" 'What's wrong, pardner?' he asked, with a trace of anger in his voice.

" 'I'm just wondering, Sands,' I replied, 'how they came to be hung up there like that. They couldn't hang themselves in suicide and the bones remain intact. Let's look closer!'

"We moved closer to the dangling relics. As I had implied, the bones were linked together with wire and hung against the wall with metal pegs!

" 'The dogs!' Sands hissed in my ear, his voice steady and as strong as a young man of twenty-five. I looked at him curiously and indeed, he was a young man again, save for his whiskers. Strangely, I thought, had we actually come upon the mythical Fountain of Youth that the early Spaniards actually believed existed in one of the Seven Lost Cities of Cibola? Were we about to find, here in Death Valley, one of those seven cities? Hardly! My imagination must be running wild, I thought.

" 'Maybe some prospector had found these deposits, Sands,' I whispered, 'and hung those skeletons there to keep others away. It's not impossible.'

" 'No,' Sands said, 'it's not impossible, but it isn't likely! Skeletons wouldn't frighten a man away from a great wealth like lies here. Your idea don't explain that crazy ball of metal, either. I think there's more to this than shows on the surface.'

" 'Perhaps you're right at that,' I acknowledged, 'but who in hell would want to hang a couple of grinning skeletons out here like that? By the way did you compare the bones?'

" 'Yes, I did compare them and I'm convinced that they are the bones of two men. Neither is a woman! They are not Allie and her father!"

"I felt better at that. Buoyed up by the discovery, Sands' never dying hope that he would still find his lost sweetheart Allie Lane, expressed itself in his features.

" 'And I feel that Allie is alive,' he continued. 'I don't know why I feel it. It might be what we call a coincidence or just a hunch, but I think we'll find her near here!'

" 'Poor girl,' I muttered.

"I expected to find the age-whitened bones of Allie Lane and her father but events seemed to have bred within me a belief such as Sands'.

IV

Into the Cavern

I FELT THAT OUR SEARCH WAS at its end when we beheld the two skeletons, but our observations told us that they were the remains of two heavy-set men, one of whom had the ball of an old time bullet lodged in his right wrist bone. We concluded that they had been a couple of frontier bandits or prospectors who wandered onto the Manalava Plain and died there of thirst. Sands strode over to the wall and lifted a skeleton from the pegs. I watched him with amazement. The rattle of the bones sounded oddly in the crater. He threw one and then the other into the pool. As we watched, intently, the bones slowly sank and vanished until there was nothing left. The stuff must have been horribly thick and viscous to retain it on the surface so long.

" 'That's about the best burial they'll ever get,' he muttered. 'I'd hate to die knowing that my bones would be hung on a wall to frighten folks away!'

"I agreed with Sands. He seemed a different man altogether from the wrinkled old gent to whom I had been accustomed. With many of his years gone, and apparently young again, he was wide-awake to the adventures at hand. Without further words, he strode lightly to the entrance of the luminous cavern. I followed, choosing to be led rather than lead.

"Carefully we picked our way into the tunnel which widened perceptibly beyond the entrance. Inside, the red glow was more pronounced. Sparkling gems, cropping out of the walls, glittered brilliantly under the red radiance. A well worn path led along the center of the cavern's floor and we followed it for perhaps a hundred yards on a downward angle of probably five or six degrees. We observed small caves branching off from the main tunnel, but we continued along the trail of the larger one.

"Suddenly, as we picked our way along the path, we heard the sounds of a dismal chant. Steadily the sound increased. The entire cavern reverberated with the ominous sound and almost from the moment it reached our ears, we found ourselves in total darkness! The entrance of the cave which had previously been open to the sun-light and looked bright and inviting from the cavern's interior, was now totally dark! The inky blackness was as oppressing as the damp, stagnant air was nauseating. I reached out and grabbed Sands' arm so that we would not get separated. At the same time I jerked my gun out of the holster. Sands grunted when he heard the click of the hammer being drawn back under the thumb.

" 'Don't shoot until you're sure what you're shootin' at, pard,' he whispered in my ear. 'I think I hear footsteps off there to the left. Get around me or let me have the hog-laig!'

" 'I hear something in back of me, Sands,' I replied, a little nervously. 'Something seems to be flyin' around our heads like bats but I don't hear the whirr of wings!'

" 'Don't move then!' he advised.

" 'That's a hell of a racket, ain't it?' I remarked, trying to control my agitation.

"We stood closer together in the blackness. The tunnel reeked with an evil odor that was sweet and lung-tickling. I have smelled something like that before in caves where wild cats had holed up, but this was a thousand times stronger.

" 'No use standing here, pardner,' Sands whispered softly, 'I can't hear any more footsteps and the bats seem to have vanished. Suppose you light up the carbide lamp. I want to look around in here but not in the dark. Might fall into a hole!'

" 'Let's stand still a few more minutes,' I said 'I'm a little uneasy about this. I want to get my bearings for a line on that opening where we came in. Looks like the hole has been closed up.'

" 'That hole couldn't be closed without us hearing it!'

" 'With that noise down below you couldn't hear it anyhow!' I argued. 'Sounds like a pack of demons thirstin' for blood!'

" 'It don't sound any too good, I'll admit that,' Sands acknowledged. 'It might be wind caused by an underground suction, or chlorine gas blowing out of a volcanic fissure. The stink smells like chlorine gas.'

"We peered into the darkness trying to penetrate a solid wall of unfathomable black. My eyes ached under the strain. I removed my hand from Sands' arm to rub them.

"Suddenly a darting light passed like a meteor through the blackness above, showering green, luminous sparks to the floor of the cave! In the brilliant light I caught sight of Sands' features. The expression on his face told me that he had barely missed being struck by the glaring missile. He yelled loudly to drop down flat, as another light in the form of a sphere apparently of molten metal, darted over us, dropping a shower of floating sparks.

"Instantly the meteor-like ball was followed by other bright, swift-moving lights which passed perilously close to us and raced to the end of the tunnel toward the entrance. Their passing was marked by a low, droning hum of a likeness to the drone of the big sphere that had been shot from the whirling column in the center of the pool.

"Lying flat on our backs on the hard lava floor of the cavern back there under the terrible Manalava Plains, Sands and I watched the space above us. Closer and closer came a steady stream of brilliant lights that permeated the already nauseating air with the odor of burning carbon!

I raised my gun several times to fire at one of the lights but thought better of it until I was sure of hitting the mark. Meanwhile I began to think what might happen should I actually succeed in striking one of them. I asked Sands' advice. He suggested that I try my luck.

"I raise my head a little to look down into the tunnel. Issuing from what appeared to be a deep hole perhaps a half mile ahead, came a spinning ball of glaring fire. It hovered for an instant over the yawning, luminous hole and then darted in our direction at a terrific speed. I lifted my gun from my hip. When the light was near enough, I pulled the trigger.

"The sharpness of the concussion filled me with fear, but in the instant the light was gone. Only a shower of sparks remained to prove that my slug had gone true. The sparks lay on the tunnel floor, glowing like lumps of molten copper, green and red.

"We lay on the ground for several minutes more. Then I nudged Sands. We walked along the path for perhaps a dozen feet and then I realized that our sense of direction was gone altogether. We were completely lost in a strange world of blackness pierced only by mysterious lights and sounds, of whose origin I could not guess.

"Presently we realized that it was folly to wander around when any step might precipitate us into unknown dangers. I had an unpleasant feeling of helpless fear that was gradually overcoming my reasoning powers again.

"At times I looked fearfully to the right and left, but saw nothing but blackness. The glowing remains of the think. Meanwhile the cavern was in pandemonium. The moaning sounds had again become a wail which gradually developed into high-pitched shrieking. I expected momentarily to see another huge whirling sphere shooting toward the entrance of the cave where we lay panic-stricken.

"To my horror, the cave began to lighten with the green luminous glow, and a score of yards beyond I saw what appeared to be a sluggish red stream, thick and mucky, flowing toward us. I kicked at Sands to draw his attention to it.

" 'I see it, pardner,' he whispered. 'What do you think it is?' "

" 'Lord!' I answered. 'If I only knew!'

" 'Let me have your lamp. I'm going to take a chance on lighting it. We've got to get out of here!'

"My blood turned cold at the mention of the carbide lamp. For the first time I learned that it was not in my hands! At my attempt to run, I thought I must have dropped the lamp with my pack. At any rate it was gone! We crawled around the floor of the cave hoping to feel it. The murky green glow in the tunnel did not help us any at all. It only added to the disguise of the cave's interior.

"Sands cursed me for a fool at allowing the lamp to drop from my hands, leaving us without a means of penetrating the darkness. My pack, which I had placed on my knees before me, when digging out our rations, was gone likewise. Nowhere could they be found. We searched the floor of the cave minutely in the sickly green light but without success.

"Suddenly the cave became brilliant with light. The

light had long since died out and the cave was once again in total darkness. There was no life, no sound, no motion except for the movements of Sands and me. Allie Lane at that time was very remote from my thoughts. I was thinking of personal safety and although I had some assurance in the feel of my gun in my hand and its effectiveness on the dangerous lights, I was nevertheless fearful. I felt the panic of utter isolation from humanity. I was in a different world entirely!

"Sands suggested again that I get out my carbide lamp. I hesitated, fearful lest our positions be clearly defined in the light, and lay us open to further danger from the fast floating lights and their sources.

"Stagnation—everything sinking and stale! The cavern smelled of sheer funk. It curled our nostrils and nauseated our stomachs to such an extent that I became violently ill temporarily.

" 'Let's get out of here, Sands!' I whispered. 'I think we are headed into the cave and if we turn around we can reach the opening.'

" 'We can try it. I'd like to get a breath of air.

" 'Hold on to me then,' I said, 'we'll get out!'

" 'Maybe!'

"With Sands holding onto my arm we turned around and began a slow, deliberate walk back to what we thought was the entrance of the cave, long since dark. For perhaps fifteen minutes we picked our way along the cave not knowing what step might sink us into death.

"Suddenly I collided with a solid wall. Around the

edges the sunlight of the outer world flickered and I knew that it was the entrance to the cave.

"We were stunned when we discovered that the entrance had been closed solidly with massive slabs of rock! The air was less heavy and stagnant here and we sat down after a strenuous effort to roll back the rock wall that trapped us. We rested, motionless on the floor of the cave. I could not see Sands but sounds of his heavy, even breathing came to me. We were too exhausted even to speak but I suddenly felt the pangs of hunger.

"I slipped my pack from my shoulders and felt within it. I handed Sands several squares of hardtack and a bar of chocolate for which he mumbled his thanks. Ravenously I devoured my ration; then got out my carbide lamp and toyed with it.

"As I sat I noticed that the low moaning sounds that we had previously heard were again issuing from deep within the cave. I shuddered. The sounds beat terrifically on my brain and in my terror I drew my gun and fired four shots rapidly toward the interior.

"Instantly the hole was a bedlam! I leaped to my feet to run but tripped over Sands' outstretched feet and tumbled to the floor.

" 'Take it easy, pardner!' Sands advised, softly, his voice quivering. At his calm words I lay down quietly.

"You cannot conceive my terror. Could I have but known the reasons and the causes for the many things we had seen and the incidents that happened, I would have been better able to control myself. Terrified, I lay on the floor of the cave and it was a long time before I was able to suddenness of the change from darkness blinded my eyes and instinctively my hands shot up to cover them. It stunned me for a moment and then I looked around.

"I stared incredulously at the sight; then turned to look at Sands. He was poised on his hands and knees, stopped by the sudden light, in his search for the lamp and the grub pack. His mouth hung open. I looked up again.

"Standing around us in a circle stood a score of the strangest man-like beings I ever beheld. They stood motion-less, surveying us. Towering high above Sands and me, the strangers looked down through great eyes that blinked slow and deliberate like owls' orbs in the night. Instinc-tively my hand shot down to my gun butt. When it neared the metal it stopped and I jerked my hand away. The gun seemed charged with powerful electricity! I managed to grin foolishly under the glare of two-score blinking eyes. Then I made a careful appraisal of the beings surrounding us.

"Tall in stature—probably seven feet high, they towered above us. With great heads void of hair, powerful bull necks, barrel chests and long skinny limbs that appeared to be of rubber like the tentacles on the weird cactus back on the Manalava Plain, the creatures to the human eye, were repulsively grotesque! Their arms, thin and sinuous, like their legs, seemed of rubber and they hung motionless at their sides. I looked for hands. There were none. At the ends of the tentacle-like arms, there seemed to be sucker-like cups like the end of an elephant's trunk!

"For several moments they stood appraising us. Like-wise we studied them. I noticed that above their heads waved two thin, flexible tubes that curled at the end and were attached to the brows just above their owlish orbs. Like the antennae on a desert butterfly, the tubes twitched this way and that! The absence of ears at the sides of their flat heads added bestiality to their repulsive features, and their mouths, like the jaws of a toad, were pointed and bony! Each had the face of a frog and all looked alike except that the creature standing nearest to me and in front of the rest, was perhaps a head taller. He wore a brightly-hued belt of metal around his narrow, skinny hips.

"The big fellow's tubes at his forehead were waving nervously. I stared at him blankly for I had a peculiar feeling that somehow he was trying to speak to me. I shot an inquiring glance at Sands. He was still in the same position. His knit brows displayed a growing uneasiness. Surely, I thought, these grotesque fellows were not hostile, otherwise they would have made short work of us!

"I crawled slowly to my feet and stood erect in front of the repellant fellow, who was apparently the leader of the frog-featured beings. His green, luminous face was tilted down to me and from it radiated the warmth of radium. He towered three heads above me and I felt like a pigmy beside him and equally as helpless.

" 'Well—,' I managed to say, in astonishment. "His tubes stood out stiff and motionless. A strange power seemed to be penetrating into my crazed brain and his attitude made me feel that he was reading my thoughts. Suddenly my brain was struck with a direct question, although I heard no voice.

" 'What are you doing here?' a strange, silent voice seemed to ask.

"In answer my thoughts asked the same question and instinctively my lips blurted out the words evasively. The awesome creature snapped his frog-like mouth and his antennae stood rigid.

" 'Answer me!' The silent demand was hostile under the glare of his owlish orbs.

"My hand hung close to the butt of my gun but I kept my fingers from touching it. My brain was a whirl of thoughts, making clear thinking impossible. There seemed to be a peculiar power continually stirring my brain, building up slowly an explanation for our presence there. I opened my mouth to speak but the strange power ordered me to keep it shut and to think. I looked around for Sands. He was standing at my side, his face as green as the ghastly faces in front of me. I felt somewhat assured by his presence and then my thoughts raced, omitting no episode of the long search by my partner for his sweetheart, Allie Lane. My thoughts told of tracing Allie and her father to the radium pool and how, on discovering the cave, we had decided to search within it for some remains of the ill-fated friends of Sands.

"In my excitement I blurted the question: " 'Has anyone here ever heard of Allie Lane—have you ever seen her?'

"The big fellow turned his tubes towards Sands as though to question him. Sands must have been thinking terrible things about the grotesque beings who stood around us, for the big fellow reached out a rubber-like arm and suddenly circled it around his neck. Jerked from his feet, Sands fell to the floor with a curse.

" 'Get him pardner!' he yelled at me. 'Shoot him!'

"The suddenness of the hostile move against my friend naturally forced me into action and in spite of the peculiar heat in the metal of my gun, I drew it from its holster and fired point blank into the big fellow's face.

"I expected to see him fall and the others dash away but the fellow merely croaked like a frog and tightened his hold upon Sands. A small, round hole appeared in his face where my slug had struck him just below the left eye. A yellow liquid that glowed like fire, trickled out of the hole for an instant, then vanished as the wound rapidly closed up! I jammed my gun into the holster, amazed and fearful.

"Instantly the circle of strange creatures tightened around us. We were doomed men, I thought, as I was roughly lifted into the arms of one of the frog-faced beings!

V

The Jovians

BOTH SANDS AND I WERE carried on the broad chests of the mysterious creatures far into the cavern. They made several abrupt descents and the oppressive air told me that we were far below the surface of the Manalava Plain! Their movements were rapid and forceful and their long skinny legs bore their weight remarkably well, although they wobbled like strutting geese. During the entire course, the tunnel was brilliant with changing colors of various hues from green to red and vermilion—everchanging.

"As I lay cradled in the tentacle-like arms of the big brute who carried me, I smelled his evil breath. The odor was the same nauseating smell that had curled our nostrils and threatened to explode our lungs on several occasions since we entered the cavern. With each slow blink of his eyelids, there was an accompanying metallic click. Occasionally he opened his toad-like mouth and when he closed it hard, bony lips snapped like the spring of a trap. Sands was being borne along by a broad-backed creature in front of me. I could see his head bobbing with each wobbly step of the beast and I knew that he was unconscious.

"I felt worried about Sands. The grip of the big fellow's arm around his throat could have broken the spine of an ox without any effort. I cursed the brutes venomously. The fellow bearing me tightened his grip around my chest and I was forced to gasp for breath. When I became quiet he loosened his hold. I felt a searing welt rise across my body.

"Presently we were carried into a great, circular chamber far below the surface of the Manalava Plain! The chamber was luminous with the strange, pale green color. In the center spun a huge glowing sphere and it was surrounded by smaller spheres, each spinning in an atmosphere of its own—like the earth—with its suns and moons revolving around it. The huge ball in the center seemed to float in air without any visible support. The smaller spheres likewise spun in mid-air at perhaps a forty-five degree angle from the large one. They emitted a high-pitched whine as they spun.

"My eyes, now accustomed to the luminous glow, searched every corner of the chamber. To the right, stand-

ing on a flat rock platform, were three massive chairs of
green metal that was studded with precious stones. The
chairs were vacant.

"Lined around the circular chamber were several hundred more of the grotesque creatures who had carried Sands
and me far into the underground world. They stood motionless as though at attention. From deep in the bowels of
the earth came a clanging of bells and each creature in
the chamber, with the exception of the two who bore Sands
and me across their chests, hung their heads. I heard the
scraping of rock against rock over to my right and I allowed
my gaze to wander there.

"A huge circular slab of rock was rolling away from
an entrance into the chamber. I watched it intently until
its removal exposed a glittering doorway. I had become so
engrossed in watching the door that I failed to notice that
I was being carried toward the platform. As I was borne
nearer to the three chairs, I observed standing in the opening the majestic figure of a huge, bestial creature, bedecked
in purple and gold robes of a metal that glistened blindingly. The fellow carrying me halted before the platform
and placed me on the floor. The tall figure in the doorway
moved quickly out of the entrance and walked stiff-legged
toward the chairs.

"From his dignity I at once accepted him as the king or
chief of the grotesque frog-men. I stood erect, my gaze
following him. He appeared not to take the slightest interest in me. I looked around as he neared what I accepted as
his throne. Sands was lying still on the broad chest of the
brute who had carried him in. His head hung loosely on his

shoulders. Disconsolately, my gaze again returned to the majestic figure on the throne. He sat stiffly, the tubes above his eyes, waving slowly. While my interest was centered on Sand's lifeless body, two other beings had followed the High Chief onto the throne and sat in the chairs on either side of him.

"To my uttermost surprise I beheld two human beings sitting beside the High Chief, one on either side! And one was a young woman, gaily adorned in brilliant robes of purple and gold! Her wealth of golden brown hair shimmered in the pale green light of the chamber. Her eyes were motionless and she looked out over the room like one in a trance. Her finely cut features and appealing blue eyes caused my pulse to beat more rapidly than ever before in all my life. My whole body tingled with exaltation. I had an impression that her features bore a distinct resemblance to some beautiful face that I had seen before. She stared straight ahead with unblinking eyes. I was unable to remove my eyes from her. Where had I seen that fascinating, clear-cut face? Whose features were they? Ah—I had it!

"Instantly I decided to look again at the photograph Sands had found in the old album back at the spring! Perhaps it was the photograph that had given me the impression of having at some past time beheld the gentle features of the girl.

"I walked unmolested, over to Sands' limp form and reached inside his vest. He was beginning to show signs of life when I brought forth the well-preserved photograph that he said was the picture of Allie Lane for whom we had been searching.

"Every owlish eye in that great assembly of unearthly beings, was riveted on me as I strode, photograph in hand, toward the platform. The dignified leader sat motionless on the throne and regarded me through saucer-like orbs. I felt, even though no sounds issued from his mouth, that he was conversing steadily with our capturers. The tubes, just above his broad forehead, waved in all directions as though catching thought waves being broadcast by the others in the chamber.

"The girl sat in stony immobility. The man on the other side of the High Chief was likewise motionless, his eyes staring straight ahead. The man was slightly wrinkled around the mouth though he looked to be no older than thirty. His jet black hair which had been freshly combed, glistened as from oil. Was this man Alfred Forsythe Lane, father of the beautiful girl whose trail led us to the edge of the radium pool? Hardly, I thought.

"At the edge of the platform I halted, photograph held up before my eyes. For a moment I was utterly stunned! The photograph showed the same delicately rounded chin, finely shaped lips and radiant blue eyes that marked the beauty of the girl in the chair! I stumbled backward a few steps in my astonishment.

"Allie Lane!' I must have shouted at the top of my lungs, for I heard a patter of feet that brought Driftin' Sands to my side. I looked at him. His face was white even under the luminous green glow that affected him.

" 'My God!' he breathed in amazement. 'It's Allie!'

"With a leap Sands jumped to her side on the platform.

"Instantly the High Chief raised an arm menacingly and a thin shaft of green light shot from the sucker-like tip at the end. Sands placed a wearied hand over his eyes, a small round spot, the color of chalk, appeared on his brow as he sank to the floor heavily. Allie Lane moved her finely shaped head with its brown hair hanging in thin wisps curled around her temples, and stared blankly at her fallen lover. She quivered slightly and raised her dainty white hands to her temples as though striving to bring a return of memory. Presently she gave it up with a shudder and continued to stare straight in front of her. The gaze rested upon me, I felt, and I shifted my own uneasily, help-lessly. The grotesque people of the underground had dis-played their protective powers on several occasions and I was aware of what my fate would be if I interfered to aid my friend. Whether Sands was dead or merely stunned I could not guess, but I accepted the former readily enough.

"Expecting momentarily to feel the tingle of radium rays carrying me into oblivion, I hung my head. I stood limply at the edge of the platform, full of sorrow over the turn of affairs. Here was Sands, at the end of a forty-year search for his lost sweetheart—the only living thing that had kept him alive—and there was Allie Lane, probably broken in mind and spirit and unable to go to him. Now, I thought, his life was snuffed out while he stood on the very verge of complete happiness. I offered a prayer to our Maker to re-unite them again and let them enjoy the happiness that was theirs by right of nature and heritage!

"I didn't think how strange it was at the time for Allie

Lane to be sitting there as fresh in the glory of youth as
she was when the photograph had been made of her back
in Kansas City forty years ago! I only knew that we had
found her. I looked at Sands. He was lying in a heap where
he had fallen. No move had been made on the part of the
giant tunnel-dwellers to aid him. Certainly I could not!
One move and I would meet with the same fate. I was not
ready to die. I strained hard to think of some way to help
him—to learn if he was dead. Some irresistible influence was
smothering all thought. It was then I realized that I was
being questioned by the High Chief on the throne. I cast a
quick glance past Allie Lane at him. His antennae tubes
were pointed straight toward me. I felt the strange power
that seemed to pass from his tubes to my mind. I shuddered
for it gave me a terrific pain at the base of my skull. Nevertheless I steeled myself for the ordeal of questioning that
I knew would follow. A peculiar feeling came over me. I
felt that I was gradually rising out of my physical body.
It was an incredible sensation. Then my brain grasped a
vibratory mental question. I seemed in a trance.

" 'You, Man of the Earth, what brings you into forbidden
country?'

"The peculiar eerie question gave me a faint feeling
that some time in the dim past I had heard it asked of me
through a similar process. I glanced down at my feet. They
were invisible. I seemed to hang, eyes only, suspended in a
murky haze. Before me, on the throne, sat the three silent
figures glowing brightly and tinged with a greenish hue.
Sands' inert body seemed to have vanished! I strove to
answer my questioner. My lips moved but I could hear no

words. My brain told me that an answer was taking definite shape, but it would not be the answer the monster sought!

" 'Forbidden country here in America?' I answered him silently. 'Why you must be crazy!'

"At that his saucer-like eyes blinked rapidly. His frog-like beak opened and a red, fiery tongue flicked out of a luminous opening that was his throat. The chamber was in stony silence. Only the click of the High Chief's huge eyelids broke the stillness.

" 'You, Man of the Earth,' the words telegraphed to my brain. 'Dare you jest with me? Do you know that I, Abaris, second in command of Jupiter and the entire Universe, have the power and the right to forbid anything or con-demn any world!'

"His words struck me as inexplicably funny. How silly and absurd, I thought, was this sudden boast of power from such a hideous, grotesque freak. Had he ever heard of the great armies of the United States that could fly over the Manalava Plain and annihilate his entire band of frog-like freaks? Hardly, I thought. I felt my lips curl up in scorn at his vanity.

" 'By what right have you to condemn and destroy?' I asked, more controlled.

"His flat beak opened in a froggish attempt to laugh. A peculiar cackling sound, issued from his cavernous throat. He seemed to be enjoying himself hugely.

" 'For a lowly creature like yourself, Man of the Earth, who is doomed, you speak strong words! What right have I to annihilate you? Why, ignorant one, I have the right by all the power of the Universe! I have the power of civilization ten million years in advance of your aboriginal powers! We, your superiors by millenniums, could condemn your earth to complete and instantaneous destruction should we so desire!"

"This lengthy message, telegraphed to my stunned brain, caused me to wonder what sort of beings these creatures were, from where they had come and what was their mission here. Certainly, the owl-eyed freak talked like a military lord. I began to feel that I was the proverbial mouse and the cat was merely playing with me for his own amusement. The strange power the High Chief had displayed in striking Sands to the floor, awed me considerably. Of a certainty, we men on earth boasted of no such strange weapons that shot pencil-thin light rays and killed instantly and silently. Perhaps this giant freak was not boasting after all.

"In spite of my sudden fears that perhaps this tribe of strange creatures might be able to bring into play powers far superior to our own, I still felt contempt and scorn for them. To have my partner—my friend in years of toil and sorrow, suddenly struck down by the beasts when he had found joy, was enough to bring out my hatred. The fact that they held captive, two human beings like myself, one a woman, under a strange influence, only piled fuel onto the fires of my fury.

" 'What have you done with my friend, O Abaris, Great and Exalted Ruler of the boundless Universe?' I sneered contemptuously. 'Such a Great and Glorious Ruler as you must take great pleasure in striking down an unarmed man!'

" 'I smite the hand that harms, Man of the Earth!' his soundless words shot back, hostilely.

" 'His was not the hand that harms, O Brave Abaris! His was the hand of love and loyalty—with a mind of sorrow and grief!'

"At this juncture I shot a glance at Allie Lane. Her profile was beautiful as she turned toward the grotesque creature sitting majestically at her side. Her eyes looked up into the owlish orbs appealingly. My heart jumped suddenly and I felt a lump rising in my throat. The High Chief Abaris looked down at her through wide lids. One of his snaky, tube-like arms writhed upward and encircled her soft shoulders. His head tubes hung drooped in apparent affection for this beautiful girl for whom Sands had spent the best part of his life in constant search. I cursed the huge beast roundly.

"I understood it now. The frightful brute had saved Allie Lane from a horrible death, and through some process unknown to man, he had retained within her the youth and beauty that was hers when he found her at the edge of the radium pool! He must have jealously guarded that youth through the passing of the years that had made Sands, her loyal suitor, an old and broken man! What was the secret of the strange process? Was it the radio-active qualities of the radium that had retained her youth as well as restored the youth of Driftin' Sands? If so, then why hadn't I gone through the same change? Then I remembered that Sands had accidentally dipped his fingers into the radium pool, burning off the tips. The radium must then have sent life-giving qualities surging through his veins and restored the worn and frayed nerves and tissue of his body! The same injection, but through a different process, I thought, must have been applied to the youthful body of Allie Lane. Her father, too, must necessarily have gone through the same procedure, else how could he have been restored to youth? Why had he been permitted to live at all? Surely, now, his years had passed the century mark!

"But, I thought, Allie Lane would have been better off had she died at the pool! With such a beast as the frog-featured Abaris constantly in her vision and showering her with his affections, a terrible life at best must have been hers! And Abaris must have read Sands' thoughts, too, before he struck the man down. He seemed to take great pride in his possession of the beautiful feminine creature, I felt, and guarded her zealously from others.

"Suddenly my subconscious mind reeled under the pressure of Abaris' strange power of mental telepathy. He rolled his great bald head aside and with owlish eyes, lanquidly regarded me. My gaze became fastened on his steadily blinking lids. Their metallic clap-clap-clap-clap as they opened and closed, sounded dismally throughout the chamber which was now lighted only with a pale green glow. The three figures on the throne, a deeper green but tinged with a brilliant red aurora, sat quietly. I wondered what had become of Driftin' Sands.

"Abaris grotesque features stood out abruptly and seemed almost as fair as Allie Lane and her father, under the mixture of colors that glowed from the green and red hues.

His great eyes bored into mine so deeply that I felt a sudden panic seize me.

" 'You, ignorant Man of the Earth, have seen the power of Jupiter, greatest and most powerful planet in the Universe!' Abaris' words, booming and unspoken, reached my mind. I thought it strange that these grotesque beings could converse in my own language and by mental process at that.

" 'Yes,' I admitted reluctantly. 'I have seen them! But do you know that one of our American bombing planes could fly over here and blow you and your crowd to hell?'

"Abaris' frog-like features parted in a grin. His throat rattled mirthfully. I stared at him, awed.

" 'Hoh, hoh, hoooah!' My mind throbbed under the force of his booming mental laugh. 'Why, lowly worm!' he shot, his tubes pointing straight at me, 'If I but minded to I could destroy your entire world with one little globule of radium!'

" 'What do you mean?' I asked with a sudden desire to learn all I could concerning these strangers and their awe-inspiring powers.

" 'Just this!' Abaris said, evenly and with sarcasm, 'We of Jupiter are so far your superiors that you are but worms in comparison. When your people were still clinging by their tails we of Jupiter had already mastered mathematics. During the years that followed and developed you to your present state, we of Jupiter mastered many sciences—one of which brings us to your world now. That is radium. We have mastered radium in all its forms and we are therefore masters of the Universe and all life in it.'

" 'Well,' I said, 'why didn't you destroy us here on earth then if you are so powerful? How did you get here on this earth if your planet is Jupiter?'

" 'We, Man of the Earth,' he said, amused, as though enjoying the mental conversation immensely and taking great pride in the vast knowledge of his people, 'we do not take life without cause, even though that life is no more to us than your reptiles are to you!'

" 'Then why did you kill my friend?' I queried, earnestly. 'Why have you held these two white people with you?'

" 'Your friend is unhurt physically, but mentally he now belongs to Jupiter! His intentions were doubtful when he leaped up here beside Eloli, whom your feeble mind refers to as Allie Lane! I should have killed him instantly!'

"I felt unable to think of anything for a moment, and I stared fascinated at the features that confronted me. I noticed that the colors in the chamber were changing again and that the lackadaisical visage of Abaris was growing more pronounced under the varying hues. His saucer-like eye-lids continued their resounding clap-clap-clap like the sound of shutters closing on a camera.

" 'I don't believe you, Abaris!' my voice suddenly raised. 'You killed him because you knew that he was Allie Lane's man by all the laws of humanity on this world!'

" 'What care we Jovians for the laws of your humanity!' Abaris' thought wave struck me sharply. 'I could have killed you both instantly! You were trespassing on forbidden ground and I therefore had the right to remove you from it!'

" 'How did you know we were here?' I asked.

" 'Our sentinels on the surface informed us of your coming long before you reached here. We had no intention of harming you unless you entered the crater!'

" 'Then that's why you hung up these skeletons out there—to scare us away, eh?' I inquïred. 'Did you think a few grinning skulls would make us run?'

" 'The skeleton of anything on this earth tends to frighten away the living!' Abaris declared, nonchalantly. 'Even a dog will run from the bones of its kind, why not you who are just a step higher intellectually than the dog?'

" 'You're a bragging cuss, aren't you, Abaris?' I shot back with contempt and sarcasm. 'You've been misinformed as to the status of the human race on this world! I could think up a better way to frighten a man than that!'

" 'We of Jupiter have many ways to frighten a man if you like to call yourself such. But you see we are not particularly interested in whether we frighten or not. You and your friend and these two humans beside me are the first to have come here since we arrived from Jupiter. We felt no need of methods to frighten others away!'

"My Lord! I thought, had these creatures come to this world from another planet at a time when we on this world were crossing the country in ox-drawn wagon trains? Had they arrived here before Allie Lane and her father wandered into the Manalava Plain?

" 'Yes, Man of the Earth,' Abaris' mental wave reached me in answer to my thoughts. 'We dropped down from Jupiter, long before your people began crossing your continent. We have been here exactly one hundred of your years and we are now ready to return to Jupiter, if that interests you. Our work here is completed. We return soon to our own world; four hundred million miles away.'

"Four hundred million miles! My mind whirled with staggering figures and I gave it up.

" 'I can understand your mathematical deductions, Abaris,' I said, 'but just the same I'm from Missouri and you have to prove to me that you covered all that space just to visit this world. It is hard to believe that any living thing can exist long enough to do it. It don't sound possible!'

" 'That's one of the failings of you Men of the Earth,' Abaris said, evenly. 'You think that everything that does not come within your scope of understanding is impossible. We of Jupiter long ago achieved immortality. But why should I, Abaris, second in command of the great Jupiter, explain to a lowly creature such as you, the vastly important facts of interplanetary travel?'

" 'You could tell me so I might inform my fellows on this earth that it was actually performed. Otherwise I'll have to call you a liar!' I said, with a false show of bravado. So far no harm had come to me, and Abaris had informed me that Sands suffered no permanent physical injury. I could afford to hold up my chin and meet on equal terms, with the grotesque frog-men of Jupiter! What were they anyhow but unreal, mechanical freaks?

" 'Well, to tell the truth, your world will never learn the secret from a Jovian, Man of the Earth!' Abaris' thought vibrations seemed to say. 'I might say that some day your scientists may evolve a medium for interplanetary travel and we of Jupiter do not intend to shorten the period of time when you will eventually try to visit us. You will not be welcome!'

" 'You're giving us a lot more credit than you have been saying was due us, Abaris,' I remarked with a grin. 'I'm glad you have come around to that. It makes me feel better to know that I'm a little more intelligent than a crawling worm.'

"Suddenly the chamber brightened under the brilliance of the powerful rays. Small spheres, spinning rapidly and glowing luminously, shot restlessly to and fro in the far end of the chamber. At the sound they made I instinctively turned to them for several seconds. When my eyes again returned to Abaris and his two human companions, they were gone! They had vanished apparently in thin air during the few short seconds my eyes had wandered around the brilliantly lighted chamber.

"Save for an inert heap lying on the throne in the same position that I had seen Sands when he had fallen, the chamber was completely deserted. The spheres continued their back and forth movement as I dashed quickly to Sands' side. At the close range I discovered that his body was tinged with the same luminous glow that I had seen out-shining the bodies of Abaris, Allie Lane and her father. Sands seemed stunned. He was breathing but his lungs functioned laboriously.

" 'Sands!' I cried, shaking him by the shoulder. 'Are you hurt?'

"From his lips issued a deep groan. I swung his inert body around for a look at his face. The color of it was a deeper green than it had been before. I stretched him out flat on his back and rubbed his numbed hands to restore his circulation, but it availed me nothing. Then I remembered that on my desert prospects I always carried a square lump of camphor in my pockets to rub on my lips when they became parched from the heat. I searched through my pockets for it and was overjoyed when I found it. It was soft and spongy.

"Quickly I massaged Sands' lips and nostrils. Whether camphor would serve in the place of the more powerful spirits of ammonia, I did not know, but you can imagine my joy when his lids suddenly fluttered and his lips parted. The camphor fumes had actually brought him out of the faint into which the powerful rays from Abaris' deadly weapon had thrown him.

"I laughed nervously. 'That's it, old timer!' I said, 'Snap out of it! The devil said he didn't hurt you! We've got to get Allie and her father out of here. These freaks are planning to get away from here in a hurry, taking Allie and her dad with them. Sit still and take it easy for a minute!'

"Sands sat very still for several minutes, his head resting in his hands. I squatted on the floor of the platform beside him, my eyes scouring every side of the circular chamber. To the right, the entrance into the chamber through which had come Allie Lane, her father and Abaris, stood open. The huge circular rock which must have weighed many tons had not been replaced over the opening.

"The most conspicuous thing in the entire chamber was the fair-sized globe in the center, resting on an axis and revolving rapidly. From the distance I could see that it was

lined with many criss-cross markings and glowed as though
containing a transparent liquid of a beautiful emerald color,
much similar to colored glass globes generally displayed
in drug store windows, in the city. Occasionally the brilliant spheres that hung, spinning in mid-air, darted suddenly toward the larger globe in the center. When one of the
smaller spheres neared it, the central ball emitted a peculiar high-pitched hum. The globes, combined with the
darting lights, gave me the impression that they must be
used by the Jovians for some astronomical purpose. The
big sphere, I thought, must represent the home planet of
the grotesque beings. What else could they be used for,
I wondered? But I was due to learn much before I got
out of there.

VI

Sands Recovers

PRESENTLY SANDS STOOD ERECT. He looked around him for several seconds, evidently to get his bearings. I watched him nervously. What had Abaris meant when he said that 'mentally Sands belonged to Jupiter?' I knew when I looked into Sands' eyes. Like fathomless abysses, his eyes glowed like sulphurous fires. The pupils had grown until they seemed to disappear into the rim entirely! He seemed to be in the same trance that had held Allie Lane's and her father's eyes staring straight ahead without apparently comprehensive powers.

"When I spoke to him he merely stared blankly, although I was certain that he understood my words. His lips moved to answer but no words formed in his throat.

"I shook him by the arm.

" 'I think,' I said to him, pointing to the opening from which Abaris had come into the chamber and into which he had doubtless vanished, 'that we had better find Allie Lane and her father if we hope to get out of here alive. You know that she's here and alive, don't you, Sands?'

"To me it appeared that he made an attempt to speak when he heard Allie's name mentioned, but he merely stared dumbly. At any rate I believed he understood what I had said.

" 'If we can get to Allie and her father without these critters knowing it,' I whispered into his ear, 'she might be able to point a way out of here. If we can get out I'll strike toward Stovepipe Wells and send a telegram to Los Angeles asking for help. I'm afraid we'll need a couple of bombing planes from San Pedro to get us out of this mess!'

"I grabbed him by the arm and hustled him toward the circular shaft leading from the chamber. He came readily enough but when I loosened the pressure on his arm he stood there, stock still. He seemed to have no will power whatever and his legs moved only because I hustled him along.

"As we entered the only open shaft leading out of the chamber, a high-pitched musical note became audible. I wondered if our movements had sounded some mysterious warning. As we continued on into the luminous tunnel that glittered with deposits of priceless gems, the musical note rose higher and higher so that it seemed to tax the sense of hearing to its uttermost. Questioningly I turned to Sands. One of his trembling hands was chafing his temples with thumb and forefinger. The sound gradually became a wail like the metallic scream we had heard before entering the cave that led down to the chamber.

"Suddenly I became aware that Sands had broken the influence that had held him! With a frenzied scream he leaped aside and away from me. I gazed in wonder at the man as he crouched like a beast at bay. I expected him momentarily to spring at my throat. But he finally recognized me and became controlled when I assured him the Jovians were not in sight. His first questions were of Allie Lane. Had he really seen her, he wanted to know, or had he been suffering from a brain fever? Was she really alive —as beautiful as ever? I assured him that she was.

" 'Lord!' he gasped, shuddering. 'That noise would drive a man insane!'

" 'Yes,' I whispered softly, 'But you ought to thank it for bringing you to your senses!'

" 'What do you mean?' he asked, blankly.

" 'Don't you know that the Big Chief of these freaks bounced you for jumping onto the platform?'

" 'I don't remember anything but that I'd seen or dreamed I've seen Allie Lane alive!' he said, disconsolately.

" 'Well,' I explained, 'The High Chief, who calls himself by the name of Abaris, didn't like the idea of you getting familiar with Allie and he knocked you out cold. I thought he killed you and he might have at that had he wanted to. I thought you were a goner!'

" 'He's got a hell of a nerve then!' he exploded, his face twitching in terrible rage that under the glow of green made him almost as grotesque as Abaris himself. 'I've loved Allie Lane all my life and now that I've found her nothing but death will stop me from having her!'

" 'We haven't found her yet, Sands,' I reminded him softly. 'She's somewhere down this tunnel! I think we ought to get to her as soon as we can. Those devils are going to leave here! Abaris'll probably take Allie with him!'

"For perhaps several hundred feet we picked our way, hugging the gem-studded walls, along the tunnel through which Allie Lane had entered the chamber. Overhead small balls of light flitted occasionally, illuminating the entire passageway. We encountered several smaller passageways branching off from the main shaft but we continued along the wider thoroughfare. What had become of the Jovians? I wondered, as we slowly edged our way along the wall. The only thing that seemed to mark their existence in the great underground maze of tunnel and caverns, deep below Death Valley, was the persistent high-pitched musical notes that smashed into the ear-drums with an unending viciousness.

"Presently our footsteps led us into another circular chamber somewhat larger than the one into which Abaris had come. This great room was illuminated by darting lights which exposed units of rapidly revolving machinery from which emanated the high-pitched musical notes!

"In our appraisal of the machinery we saw what appeared to be perhaps a half dozen cylindrical tubes that stood upright, spinning rapidly. Over each glowed a pale green luminosity. The bases of the cylinders went through the hard rock floor of the chamber and their spinning movement created a terrific suction, for the air in the cavern was swirling. Attached to each of the cylinders were hundreds of small tubes that gave off a deep green ray for their entire length. One tube ran from the cylinders to a central manifold to which was attached a larger tube that fairly sputtered and glowed under a force similar to but more powerful than a great vacuum tube.

"Audible even above the noise that was created by the rapid whirl of the peculiar machines, came the steady, rhythmic throb of centrifugal pumps. The throb was the same sound that we had heard while we stood for the first time on the rim overlooking the crater containing the radium pool.

"Lights floated above the spinning machinery. They made little bright spots in the luminous green that formed the drafty atmosphere, like lanterns being swung rapidly in a murky fog. I turned to Sands who was standing just behind me staring over my shoulder, intently watching the motion of the machinery and the darting lights.

" 'I'm beginning to believe Abaris now,' I whispered in his ear. 'These devils are actually draining this world of an unknown radium deposit! All this machinery, the spheres and lights must be operated by radium power of intensity that is not possessed in the small quantities that we have found so far!'

" 'Well that might be so, pardner,' Sands placed his lips close to my ear, 'But I'm interested in Allie Lane, nothing else! Let's find her!

"I gave him an assuring nudge and we edged our way along the wall of the circular chamber, maintaining a safe distance from the whirling machinery for it seemed possessed with a powerful magnetism. I would like to have studied it closer, but something seemed to warn me to remain a safe distance away from whirling cylinders which spun like electrical generators with the tubes connected like generating brushes.

"I was still awed over the sudden disappearance of the Jovians and felt that their absence spelled some sinister disaster to us. I momentarily expected some of them to appear and seize us.

"Suddenly we came to an exit shaft just high enough to admit a Jovian, without bending. I raised an arm to estimate the height of the ceiling. My fingertips just scraped it. The tunnel was in total darkness and this appeared to be the only exit from the chamber with the exception of the one through which we had entered. We clung, hand in hand, as we went into it. We had not gone more than a dozen steps until we were enveloped in an inky blackness. Certainly, I thought, the Jovians must be aware, through their peculiar mental telepathy, that we were exploring their secret chambers. Why didn't they swoop down upon us and challenge our progress? Perhaps, I thought, they did not figure it worthwhile, believing that we would eventually lose ourselves in the network of underground vistas, tunnels and chambers, and die as the result. It was a grim outlook for both of us at best, but I had one thing—the assurance of Abaris himself, that the Jovians had no intention of harming us seriously.

"Eventually we became somewhat accustomed to the inky blackness of the tunnel and we were able to make out the forms of each other. Staring straight ahead I discovered what I accepted to be a small circular hole through which came a faint luminosity. We made for it as rapidly as we could, although we were extremely cautious and fearful lest we step into one of the bottomless abysses which I felt existed in the underground world.

"We edged our way along the tunnel for perhaps a quarter of a mile before we eventually came to the circular light which we had seen. I was not surprised when we found that it was an entrance or an exit of another chamber! We approached it carefully not knowing what might lie ahead. We had no intention of exposing ourselves to the ire of Abaris could we help it. We wanted to find Allie Lane and her father—now that he too was alive! I crawled on hands and knees to the tunnel outlet. Sands was on the opposite side of the hole. We peered intently into the chamber which was brilliantly lighted. The white brightness of the light gave me an impression that it emanated from the sun! It blinded us temporarily.

"The chamber was decorated gorgeously in purple and gold drapes that hung suspended from the room's walls. Massive metal chairs, like the three on the platform back in the first chamber, stood in artistic positions. On one side of the wall, draped with a yellow cloth of metal that glistened like fire in the brilliant light, hung a great sheet of glass-like material that mirrored other objects in the chamber. Under it stood a golden dressing table at which was a frail silver bench. Truly, I thought, as I surveyed the mirror, vanity and bench, these objects could be of no use to anyone except a beautiful woman! The thought gave birth to another idea. Perhaps this was the room to which Allie Lane had been confined!

"My eyes wandered to the far end of the chamber. To

my surprise there stood, near the wall, a massive couch that seemed to have been hewn from a great emerald block. Its coverings were of a soft, silken material, edged with gold! As I stared at the beautiful piece my eyes detected a slight movement of the coverings. I looked on the couch awe-struck.

"There before our very eyes, and apparently alone, lay Allie Lane on the silken covered, emerald couch! From underneath her brilliant robes protruded a dainty foot and ankle. Her face lay buried in her arms and her body wracked with silent sobs, her brown hair shimmering in the glare of the light. I looked at Sands, across the tunnel outlet.

"He stared intently at the reclining figure, his mouth agape. He allowed a hand to run nervously across his brow as though to gain assurance that his eyes were not playing him false. Then I made a careful scrutiny of the chamber to make certain that Allie was alone.

" 'Sands!' I hissed, in low undertones that could not have been heard beyond the few feet that separated us. 'There's your chance! There's Allie Lane on that couch, sobbing for you! Go to her, partner! I'll stay here and watch!'

"Sands looked at me for an instant, then taking my hand he squeezed it until my fingers ached.

" 'Thanks, pard!' was all he said, but his eyes showed what words would fail to tell. Releasing his grip on my hand he stepped softly into the chamber, and strode lightly with a buoyant step, toward the silken couch. A lump rose in my throat as I watched him moving swiftly toward

the girl he had gone through hell to find. Few men would
have remained loyal as he to this slip of a girl and hunted
in every nook of California for more than forty long, weary
years! It was his great love for her in the first place, his
beautiful sense of loyalty, that had caused me to join him
in the last few years of his search. Now he was at her
side!

" 'Allie! Allie!' his voice, softly appealing, came to me
where I squatted, silently guarding the chamber. My eyes
wandered around the room, nothing escaping them. Again
came Sands' appealing call. I looked at him as he stood
beside the couch, arms outstretched. The girl lay perfectly
still now, and her face remained buried in her arms as
though fearful to look up. Slowly her head turned. From
where I squatted, I could see her profile as it turned towards
Sands, tears like pearls, streaming down her cheek. I expected to see again her sweet features staring mutely blank
as they were when I first beheld her.

"Suddenly the girl sat upright and turned her face up
to Sands! Her eyes widened in amazement and fright.
I watched her closely, temporarily forgetting my own sworn
duty to stand guard over the chamber. Would she recognize her lover of forty years ago? I wondered if she really
would. Or was she still under the spell of some strange
Jovian trance? My blood pounded at my temples in those
few seconds of uncertainty. I could imagine her amazement at seeing Sands but I could not comprehend her de-
lay in flying to his embrace if she still loved him. She
sat very still, staring up into Sands' luminous green features with their month's growth of beard. Perhaps his

radium affliction and his beard had puzzled her I thought. That was true. She did not recognize him immediately as the result. For long minutes she stared at him through glistening tears.

"Then with a soft cry Allie Lane literally flew into his arms. Sands squeezed her close to him, his face buried in her tumbled brown hair. A feeling of exultation and of triumph surged through my whole body and I slapped my thigh with joy. I was immensely happy! But my joy was short lived. I always was more or less of a crank and my happiness soon fled before a cloud of gloom that formed sinister thoughts in my brain.

"Now that Sands and Allie Lane were together again, how were they to escape from the underground outpost of Jupiter? If we did succeed in finding our way out of the maze of tunnels, how did we expect to traverse Death Valley without water? It was impossible! Better had we all remain hidden far below Death Valley's burning surface than to expose ourselves to the sinister power of Abaris or the terrible fatal heat of the surface!

"Meanwhile my attention was drawn again to the two lovers as they stood beside the silken couch. Allie nestled close to the broad, powerful chest of her sweetheart and spoke to him in a low, musical voice. Quickly I glanced around the room trying not to listen to them. I had already a violent feeling of being an intruder on their reunion.

" 'Oh, Robert!' her voice, tense with both fright and joy. 'How did you ever find me—why did you risk your life to come here in the midst of these terrible creatures? I'm so afraid!'

" 'I love you, Allie!' Sands whispered affectionately. 'I love you better than life itself! I've searched for you for many years and I would have continued searching until I could no longer crawl! At last I have found you, Allie, and I shall never leave you again!'

" 'Why, Robert!' she suddenly exclaimed. 'You haven't searched for me for many years! You couldn't have because you are just the same Bob Sands you were when you started to California. Why did you let those terrible whiskers grow? I don't like them.' Allie emitted a little musical laugh; then continued. 'You must shave those horrible whiskers off at once!'

" 'Don't you know, Allie dear, that you have been lost from me for over forty years? I've been searching so long that I've lost track of time.' Sands whispered softly, looking into her expressive eyes. A smile played at the corners of her lips.

" 'You are fooling, Robert,' she said, searching his face for proof of jest. 'It just couldn't be! Why Robert I'd be an old woman now if it were true—I'd be almost sixty.'

" 'Good Lord!' I gasped to myself as I stood guard over the chamber and this secret love tryst between Allie Lane and Driftin' Sands. Didn't she know that she's been lost to the world for over forty years? Poor girl! Sands oughtn't to tell her! Then, again, it might be best for her to know everything!

"I listened intently, for now I wanted to learn any information that Allie might give to Sands regarding the grotesque Jovians and their plans. The information might aid us materially in finding ways and means of escaping them.

VII

How to Escape?

SHE WAS CRYING SOFTLY, 'IT's hard to believe you Robert! I know that you wouldn't lie to me—but it does seem impossible. Why I'm just the same as I was when you left me back in Kansas City—I don't seem to have grown older! Let me look at myself, please dear?'

"Allie walked with faltering steps over to the huge mirror hanging on the wall, and stared into it, her hands wandering softly over her features. Sands walked to her side and peered into the radium reflector. The reflection he witnessed there caused him to leap aside. For the first time he saw his face since the radio-active qualities of the radium had restored his youth. Here he was, in reality an old man who had been suddenly returned to youth. And instead of seeing the visage of a wrinkled and weather-beaten old man he beheld the features of Robert Sands as they were when he arrived in California forty years before! His was a surprise beyond description of words. He ran a hand over his face incredulously.

"Taking this opportunity to attract his attention, I whistled softly. He looked up with a jerk and patting Allie lightly on the shoulder, he came to the entrance of the tunnel where I squatted. Allie was staring into the mirror, incredulously, as though unable to believe that under ordinary circumstances she would be in the autumn of life on this earth—that the beautiful face in the mirror would long ago have become wrinkled and shrunken!

" 'Hadn't we better get Allie's father and try to get out of here, Sands?' I asked him. 'Those devils might show up any minute!'

" 'I plum forgot about you, pardner,' he said, apologetically. 'I forgot about everything. Have you any idea how we're going to get out of here? I haven't! Maybe Allie knows of some way. I'll ask her.'

" 'Yes, ask her now,' I advised. 'It's now or never!'

"With that he walked back to Allie. At the scraping sound of his boots she turned to him, smiling joyously.

" 'Allie dear,' I heard him whisper, 'I brought a friend of mine here. He's standing guard to warn us if anyone comes. I've got him in this terrible predicament and I want to get him out—get you and all of us out of here. You want to go with me back to civilization, don't you dear?'

" 'I will go anywhere with you, Robert,' she said, placing her hands on his chest endearingly.

" 'Then, dear, can you tell me how to lead us out?'

" 'I know of only one way to get out of here, Robert,' she whispered, 'but Abaris has guards there constantly. I'm afraid we could not get through them. You needn't be afraid of Abaris, Bob dear. He has been very kind to me and daddy.'

" 'Humph!' Sands snorted curtly. 'He has not been so nice to me! I'd like to blast him to hell! He knocked me cold when I first saw you, Allie, out there on the throne!'

" 'You saw me there, Robert?' she asked. 'And Abaris harmed you when you came near me?'

" 'He did, Allie! Knocked me plumb out and nearly killed me!'

" 'The brute!' she said, angrily. 'Well, maybe we'll find a way out of here, Robert! Let me call father. He's in the room next to me. Wait here!'

"Sands returned to the tunnel and squatted in the semi-darkness beside me. He was breathing hard with excitement, and there was a twinkle of joy and anticipation that formed crows' feet at the sides of his eyes. He seemed suddenly a very joyous man and forgetful of the sinister danger that hovered over all of us. What would happen, I wondered, if Abaris suddenly came upon the secret love tryst of Sands and his sweetheart? Would he fly into a sudden rage and destroy us with his terrible, invisible weapon that shot green, pencil-thin rays and killed instantly? We sat silently, Sands with his thoughts of love and happiness—I with thoughts of danger and death.

"Presently we heard a sound like the scraping of feet. Sands and I shrank close to the tunnel's wall in the semidarkness. Our fears fled, however, when Allie came into the chamber followed by her father. Lane appeared, at close range, to be a man of about forty. His hair was black and his eyes were gray and penetrating. His carriage was that of a man in his prime of life, full of power and vigor and his eyes flashed as they searched Allie's room nervously. Sands got to his feet and walked slowly into the lighted chamber. Lane stopped abruptly and surveyed him with an incredulous stare. Suddenly he stepped swiftly to Sands' side, their hands met firmly.

" 'I'd given up all hope of ever seeing you again, Bob,' he said in a clear voice that tingled with excitement. 'It' is indeed, a pleasure to have you with us again. I'm sure Allie is glad.'

" 'Thanks, Mr. Lane!' Sands returned. It's been a long time, but I've struggled hard for this meeting. You've faired well under conditions—you and Allie, but we've got to get away from these frog-faced freaks here. Tell me what you know about a way out and we'll start at once.'

" 'Just like you, Bob,' Lane said, admiringly. 'You always did want to be the first to get started. Let's sit down and talk it over. I'm terribly afraid that we'll find it hard to get out, however.'

" 'I've gone through a lot,' Sands whispered. 'A little more wouldn't amount to much. '

" 'Maybe not, Bob,' Lane interjected with a frown. 'But this is one time when you do not know what you are up against. As much as I'd like to get back home to my friends, I can't see any definite way to escape. But I'll co-operate to the fullest for yours and Allie's sake.'

"The three of them walked softly to Allie's silken couch and sat down, Allie close to Sands, his arms about her waist. I heard a faint sound issuing from the tunnel that led from Lane's chamber. I held my breath in fear. Was Abaris or some of his Jovians coming upon the scene? My blood pounded as I listened with my hands cupped behind my ears to magnify any sound. No more sounds came and I breathed easier. I turned again to the three in Allie's room. Lane was speaking, his voice, in muffled tones, reached me.

" 'Allie explained to me how you came to be here, Bob,' he was saying, 'so we won't recount it again. These strange people here claim they are from the planet Jupiter and came here solely for the purpose of obtaining a great supply of radium. It seems that they have exhausted the supply on their own planet. Through delicate instruments, Abaris says, their scientists discovered that this earth contained a great deposit of the metal. They henceforth set out to get it because life on their planet depends upon it for existence. If Abaris fails, it means that perhaps the entire population of Jupiter will be wiped out unless some other heavenly body is found to contain a deposit.'

" 'How the devil did they ever get here?' Sands asked, interestedly.

" 'I'm coming to that now, Bob,' Lane continued, softly. 'It sounds quite impossible but it is a fact that Abaris and his henchmen left Jupiter in a great spherical machine similar to some of the spheres that you probably saw on your way in here. This sphere, which is capable of inter-stellar travel, propelled by a radium process known only to their mechanics, is ready at this minute to return to Jupiter with the greater stock of that metal. For a long time they have been pumping radium out of the earth and sending it to Jupiter in small spheres which are controlled and guided by an unknown source of power. Abaris says that the deposit here is about exhausted and the cylinder pumps are bringing up the last drops of radium existing in this earth!'

" 'Abaris expects to halt the pumps very soon and enter the interplanetary sphere for departure to Jupiter! He has said that we were to accompany him to his planet and being unable to escape Allie and I have resigned ourselves to whatever fate is in store for us. I must admit that Abaris has been very good to us and while we would certainly like to get back to our people, I hold no animosity against him, except, of course, that his appearance, as are all the rest of his kind, is horrifying to us. But we have become adapted to the environment, yet we must naturally rebel against being spirited away from this glorious world of ours—to perhaps be regarded on Jupiter much in the same manner as we have looked upon strange animals here.

" 'For sometime I have suspected that Abaris in his grotesque way, is exceptionally fond of Allie! She has wanted for nothing. Her every wish has been granted, but he will not consent to our appearing before the multitude unless we submit to being placed under a strange power. In other words we are forced to undergo hypnotism for a reason that I have not been able to learn. That is why we did not see you when you stood before the platform in the throne chamber.

" 'As Allie told you, there is one exit from this underground world and that is guarded constantly either by the Jovians themselves or their grotesque death-dealing mechanical guards in the shape of a cactus tree with arms like an octopus. The mechanical Jovians seem to have all the powers of the creatures themselves, lacking only their mental faculties. Unless controlled by a living hand they are helpless.

" 'These Jovians are really geniuses in all forms. You have seen the series of spheres in the throne room with the large hall in the center. The large sphere is Jupiter in a miniature orbit. The small spheres are its moons, as *good* Abaris explained to us. Through these they are able to watch the progress of their radium spheres as they shoot their way toward Jupiter. The large spheres show their passage very plainly. But these explanations of Jovian objects and scientific genius are not getting us to our goal. So let us consider the possibility of escape. I have a plan that we may be able to use.'

"I listened intently to the plan of possible action as Lane outlined it to Sands. Allie's father explained that at a certain time the guards at the only avenue of escape would be changed and the mechanical Jovians with their tentacle-like arms, controlled by a remote central, would be put in their places. Lane explain how he had previously located the source of control over the mechanical men and was therefore, perhaps, in the position to disconnect the controlling system and suspend their activity. This sounded like a very excellent plan, but how, I thought, would it be possible for us to steal near the central control apparatus in our attempt to disconnect it? Surely, the Jovians must maintain a constant guard over such delicate and important apparatus. But on the other hand, they may not feel a need of it in view of the fact that Allie Lane and her father had been with them so long that they accepted them as being harmless.

"At any rate, Sands approved of the plan and it was decided that the attempt to escape would be made at a time when Lane was to give a low whistle and we would all meet in Allie's chamber, providing, of course, that the way was clear. Lane, with his forefinger, drew an invisible outline, showing the tunnel through which we were to go. Sands watched him closely and absorbed the information. Meanwhile, I shot rapid glances around the chamber in its entirety in my part as guard. Several times my heart jumped when I heard sounds that softly broke the stillness of the cavern, but the sounds failed to bring what I expected—the grotesque Jovians.

"Sands was standing in the center of the room now, Allie Lane in his arms. They kissed endearingly. Allie's father paced the floor nervously. Suddenly Lane stopped pacing and faced his daughter and her lover. He opened his lips to say something, thought better of it, then turned resounding snap. I expected him momentarily to bring into play his terrible, invisible ray of death. His skinny, tube-like legs held up his barrel-shaped body admirably, I thought, as I watched him from my hiding place. They seemed like stilts, unjointed except at the hips, around which was draped a narrow breech cloth of gold-edged purple. His body glistened oilily and around his bald, misshapen head rested a thin metal band, glowing luminously green. His antennae tubes waved angrily.

" 'Eloli goes with Abaris to Jupiter!' Abaris thundered, his vibrations reaching me sharply. I shuddered under the force of his powerful thought waves. 'On Jupiter we have specimens of many planetarial beings. Our scientists would like to study specimens of the aborigines of this planet. Therefore the three of you will accompany me to Jupiter! Eloli comes as the bride of Jove!'

" 'We would die there, O Abaris,' Lane parried, dejectedly. 'We of this earth could not adapt ourselves to your environment!'

" 'You do not seem to understand, Man of the Earth,' Abaris' vibrations said, 'that we of Jupiter have accomplished immortality. There is no death on Jupiter! Will you come voluntarily or shall I be forced to resort to other methods?'

"From where I lay hidden in terror, I watched Sands' face. In his anger his features twisted with fury. I could not help him should he attempt to attack the huge Jovian commander who stood before him. If I only could, how gladly I would have gone into the chamber!

"Suddenly I heard a dismal hooting from somewhere

half away. He swung around presently as though he had decided on some question confronting him, and spoke softly.

" 'Allie,' his words, nervous and tense, reached me. 'You love, Bob, don't you dear?'

" 'As well as life, father,' she answered. Sands turned to look at Lane, puzzled.

" 'Suppose, then,' Lane returned, 'that you marry Bob now. It would be a good thing in the face of whatever confronts us.'

" 'I would marry him now, father,' Allie said in a half whisper that I barely caught. 'But how?'

" 'You forget, my dear, that I was a minister back in Kansas City,' her father smiled.

" 'I've waited a long time, Allie,' Sands put in, holding Allie's shoulder and looking into her eyes lovingly.

" 'Then I will marry you at once, Robert,' she said, her eyes shining with happy tears. 'Father can perform the ceremony.'

"Fascinated, I watched the procedure that followed, forgetting my duty as guard in whose hands must rest the lives of the happy three. With my eyes and attention on Allie as she whispered 'I do,' I failed to notice that Abaris had suddenly come to the entrance of the chamber and was standing there silently regarding the trio. Lane was saying 'I now pronounce you man and wife,' when I beheld Abaris' towering form as he stood menacingly just inside the room. The tubes of his forehead stuck out rigidly, his tentacle-like arms twitching in anger, and his owlish eyes opened and closed rapidly. I shrank back into the darkness of the tunnel, fearful, lest I be discovered. From my hiding place, however, I could see the entire chamber.

"As though struck by some terrific force, Sands and Lane at once spun around and faced Abaris. Allie emitted a fearful little cry and shrank back against the wall. Abaris' tubes were pointed at them menacingly and I knew that he was speaking to them in his peculiar mental telepathy. What words flew between them I was not able to catch for I had learned that I could not receive the wave vibrations unless the tubes were pointing directly at me.

"Suddenly I heard Sands' words as he angrily informed Abaris that Allie had just become his wife and that it was no man's business what he was doing in the chamber with her. His features twitched with growing anger as he spoke, his hands were clenched.

" 'You, frog-face!' I heard him shout, 'I've searched for Allie Lane for forty years! Now that I have found her and she has become my wife, you nor anyone else can take her away from me alive!'

" 'Eloli is the bride of Jupiter, Man of the Earth!' I caught the thunderous vibrations from Abaris' tubes which now waved spasmodically in all directions. His thoughts were so powerful that they carried to me where I crouched.

" 'Allie Lane is my wife!' cried Sands, hotly. 'We die before she goes with you to your planet of crazy freaks!'

" 'Yes, O Abaris,' Lane put in, weakly, shaking as one palsied. 'Allie is this man's wife. You cannot take her away from him. It is the law of humanity!'

"Abaris' frog-like beak opened and then closed with a

behind Abaris, that gradually grew nearer. I watched the opening of the tunnel behind him expecting momentarily to see his followers enter the room. Two abreast they came, their bodies shining with freshly applied oil, their loins covered with shimmering breech-cloths. Unlike Abaris, they wore no bands around their huge heads. Like soldiers, their line broke in the center where Abaris' huge body stood like a pivot, and they single-filed around the walls of the circular chamber.

"I shot a quick glance at Sands. He stood belligerently watching. Allie had crept into his arms and buried her head against his bosom. Lane stared down at the floor, downcast and utterly dejected. When I first beheld Lane, I was impressed with his flashing eyes and strong, powerful body and had figured upon his co-operation at such a dire moment as this. But perhaps, I thought, he realized unlike Sands and myself, the utter futility of objecting to the demands of the Jovians. But Sands was of a different mettle.

"Slowly he moved Allie behind him and again faced Abaris. The Jovians lined around the chamber wall, stood apparently at attention. They made no move to interfere. Had Abaris ordered them to remain inactive, relying upon his own power of combat to force the three humans into submission?

" 'Frog-face!' Sands shouted, insultingly, at Abaris. 'You call off your dogs and we'll settle this right now! I'm not afraid of your crazy lights and even if I was I'd rather die than submit to you!'

"Abaris' throat cackled with his peculiar laugh. His owlish eyes stared through unblinking lids. Sands approached him with sinister steadiness, crouched ready to spring at the bull-like throat of the giant. I stared at him fearfully. Here was the end, I thought, as Abaris tilted his huge head to look down upon his insignificant antagonist. I glanced around the chamber at the froggish Jovians. They continued to stand silently at attention.

VIII

The Struggle

As I watched the unfolding of the terrible scene in the chamber, I found myself wondering what I would do if Sands actually attempted to fight his way through the death-dealing rays of the Jovians. My hand accidentally touched my gun butt and for the first time since I had used the weapon back in the first tunnel, I remembered that I still possessed it. I felt somewhat heartened at the reassuring touch but how useless it was in fighting the grotesque frog-men from the distant world! Surely it could not kill or disable them for hadn't

I thumbed a slug into the bony features of one of them?
That slug would have killed a man instantly, but the Jovian had no more than croaked as the lead tore through
his head!

"I patted the gun affectionately and inspected the cylinder. Reloading I snapped it back into its holster with a
grim determination that I would use it! Better had Allie
Lane, her father and Driftin' Sands rest in peace on this
earth, than in mortal terror forever on Jupiter, I thought!

"Suddenly my eyes were brought back to the chamber
by a curdling scream. Allie had fainted as Sands sprang
at the bull-like throat of Abaris, upsetting him in the suddenness of his attack. Lane stood petrified, Allie lay unmolested and unaided upon the floor.

"Just inside the chamber near the entrance, Sands and
Abaris seemed locked in a terrible embrace of death. Chest
to chest they lay on the floor, Sands on top, holding in his
powerful hands the thin, rubber-like arms of the hideous,
bestial-visaged ruler of the Jovians! Sands grunted as he
strained hard to hold Abaris' flexible arms to prevent him
from bringing into play the terrible weapon that seemed to
be concealed in the sucker-like tips at their ends. It seemed
like the conflict of two great forces—man and beast—in a
terrible battle for supremacy—like good and evil, angel
and demon. I was thrilled at the great heroism of Sands
and my heart swelled with the pride of having his loyal
friendship. Slowly I edged my way toward the chamber,
keeping well against the wall, for a closer view of the
struggle. As uneven as it seemed, Sands, I thought, was
the better of the two physically. But how could he hope to

win such an unequal combat, unarmed, and against the terrible green death rays of Abaris? White man and plane-tarial beast! No greater contrast could be imagined.

"The muscles in Sands' neck bulged as he labored to hold the tough, flexible arms of Abaris. The Jovian's skinny legs, unjointed and stilt-like kicked spasmodically, poor protection against Sands' powerful limbs. From a better point of vantage I watched the struggle. Which of the two would win the terrible battle of physical forces?

"Suddenly Abaris gave a great heave that cast Sands clear from his barrel-like body! But Sands held, with bull dog tenacity, onto the writhing arms of the Jovian leader, struggling vainly to prevent Abaris from aiming his pencil-thin emerald rays of destruction. Once Abaris shot his terrible ray and a Jovian near him vanished entirely in a puff of acrid smoke! A ray struck one of the huge chairs and it crumbled. This combat, I felt, would be more like a wrestling match due to the fact that it seemed impossible for Abaris to rise on his stilt-like legs. That much in favor of Sands! But what would happen to him if Abaris succeeded in striking him with a green ray shot with un-controllable anger?

"I studied Abaris' bestial features to see how he was accepting the terrific throttling he was receiving. His owl-ish orbs gleamed, flaming red, and stared bestially into Sands' set features, his terrible power of will burning into the man's brain. I cast a quick glance at Allie. She was just recovering from her faint and her father was at her side. From behind fluttering lids, Allie looked at the struggling figures, thrashing about on the chamber floor. She groaned softly and hid her face, sobbing.

"Watching them my muscles involuntarily became tense. My breath came in gasps born of sheer sympathy for Sands and his long lost sweetheart.

"Slowly, very slowly, the dominating will power of Abaris overcame the struggling physical force of Sands. Gradually he eased his terrible grip on the Jovian's writhing arms, and steadily Abaris was bringing their sucker-like tips toward his antagonist. Realizing his waning strength, Sands made a desperate effort to tear his eyes from the blazing, relentless orbs of Abaris, turning his head to the side. But struggle as he would, with all the physical strength at his command, he could not check the gradual domination of brain-power and will that was slowly but surely smothering him to submission.

"Presently Sands' muscles relaxed and finally the terrific power of Abaris' dominating will swept into the core of his brain, overpowering him. I cursed softly and hid my face in my hands for a second.

"Sand's head dropped to one side, his powerful arms hung limply. Blood streamed from his nostrils, caused by his tremendous physical efforts. I caught a glimpse of his eyes as his head fell. They were stark, unseeing eyes! His body shuddered convulsively as it slipped inertly to the chamber floor. Abaris was hoisted erect by two of his Jovians, his tubes waving victoriously, a cackling laugh in his throat.

"Allie Lane screamed and her father stroked her shaking head gently as Abaris strode, wobbling like a duck, toward them. I looked at Sands. His breathing was heavy and irregular. Abaris, I thought, had not killed him outright, nor had he brought into play his terrible rays. His great mental power alone had completely subdued him.

"Slowly my hand stole to the butt of my gun. With a jerk I snapped the weapon out of its holster, holding back the hammer with my thumb. In a space of several seconds I could have hurled five slugs at Allie and her father and the inert form of Sands. The sixth, I had planned, was to crash through my own brain. I levelled the gun at Allie's temple exposed through a wisp of her soft, brown hair, but I could not find the heart to release my thumb from the hammer. Suddenly I felt a wave of great remorse surge deep within me for not sending a half dozen shot into the owlish eyes of Abaris. Why hadn't I shot him as he lay there on the ground struggling under Sands, and clipped the writhing arms from his body? Was I actually the kind of a coward who would stand by, hiding like a frightened jack-rabbit while the life was being crushed out of my dearest and most loyal friends?

"A terrible rage filled me. What would my wife think of me back at Balch if she learned that I had stood idly by like a whipped cur and permitted those uncouth freaks to commit a wrong against Allie and her lover? How could my children ever live down the cowardice of their father! It was with these thoughts in my maddened brain that I suddenly dashed out of the tunnel, gun in hand, and blocked Abaris' passage toward Allie and her father. I felt a terrible urge to kill—to spill the blood or whatever it was that coursed through the veins of the frog-faced beasts!

" 'Stop, Abaris,' I shouted hysterically. 'Stop where you are! I'll kill you if you move!'

"He stared at me through flaming, owlish orbs. His frog-like mouth opened and there came from his cavernous throat the mocking, cackling laugh. It was maddening— his cackling indifference! Suddenly remembering that it was within the power of these strange creatures to render my weapon useless, causing it to heat and burn my hand, I lifted the barrel from my hip and let fly. Swiftly and with the flaming desire to kill pounding at my brain I thumbed the hammer of my gun! In a row, six round, green holes appeared just above Abaris' flaming eyes! He tottered for an instant and then recovered himself. An emerald green liquid poured from the holes and ran down into his owlish eyes.

"So rapidly were the slugs hurled from my gun that the Jovians did not instantly grasp their significance. Then abruptly the entire chamber seemed alive with thin green rays that played with deadly precision around me. Abaris, suddenly ill from the effect of the six slugs passing through his head, made a weak attempt to lift a tentacle-like arm. It was with an effort that he brought it up. I made a leap at him but I was too late. A ray shot from the tip of his fiendish arm! I felt a tingle on my left side, just over the heart. The chamber floor seemed to rush up as I fell, heavily. For several seconds I lay there, in full command of my faculties but unable to move a muscle. My head swam and I had a feeling that I was being hurled through

space at a terrific speed. Then a terrible blackness overcame me and I seemed to be falling into a yawning abyss.

"How long I lay there I do not know. For ages, it
seemed, I lay on my back making no attempt to move, but
staring into an inky blackness overhead. What had caused
the chamber to become dark, I wondered? Were my eyes
really open? I pinched myself. I was not dead after all!
I listened attentively for some sound to indicate the presence of someone. I heard nothing. The silence was awful. Then I wondered if I had succeeded in killing Abaris.
If so, he should be lying at my feet. With an effort I
wiggled a leg in an attempt to feel the floor near it. Perhaps Abaris had crawled away, or his men had removed
him from the room, I thought. Then I remembered the
futility of trying to kill a Jovian!

"I felt no pain although the blood pounded at my temples and I felt terribly weak and nauseated. My left side
seemed numb—deadened where Abaris' ray had struck.
Presently as I lay in the darkness, my ears caught a low
moaning sound. Increasing in volume, the sound soon became a high-pitched wail like that which we had heard
when we beheld the sphere whirling on the column in the
center of the radium pool. My ear drums pounded under
the force of the shriek and I placed my hands over them
to shut out the maddening sound.

"Suddenly the whole earth seemed to tremble! A rumble filled the room as though the world were in the tumul-
tuous throes of some great upheaval! With an ominous
roar the floor under me shuddered and cracked. I lay panic
stricken, thinking that a terrible earthquake had swept over

the Valley of Death.   Crashing earth-slides roared around
me as I lay helpless.   Overhead I could see a thin streak
of light penetrating through a fissure that was slowly wid-
ening!   The chamber was becoming brighter under the
glare of light that entered it from the fissure.   I stood upon
my feet and braced myself to keep from falling under the
swaying movements of the earth.   I looked around quickly.
The chamber was entirely vacant.   Not a sign remained of
Abaris, his Jovians, Allie or any of them!   They were gone!
At my feet I noticed a spreading pool of green liquid.   I
cursed Abaris and his hideous followers roundly.

"Presently as I stood staring down at the liquid that
must have poured from the wounds I had inflicted upon
Abaris, I heard a terrific roar coming from somewhere near.
The floor of the chamber rolled like the surface of an angry
sea.   I was dashed against the wall where I lay.   I expected
momentarily to see the chamber close up and crush me to
death, sealing me in a living tomb deep beneath the Manalava Plain!

"There came a terrific, thunderous crash, the impact of
which caused me to rise from the ground and fall again
yards away!   With the crash came the blinding flash of
some terrible explosion.   A great, hissing sound reached
my ears and then I heard a loud, ear-splitting shriek.   I
looked overhead at the fissure in the earth through which
filtered the soul-gladdening sunlight.   I caught a glimpse
of a great sphere travelling at a terrific speed into the sky!
As it sped away, the shriek of its passing became less discernible and soon died out altogether.   The Jovians had
departed for their own planet, taking Allie Lane, her father

and Driftin' Sands with them! Gradually the earth roar ceased and with it ceased the earth's heaving.

"I stared around me now able to see the entire chamber. Not an object remained in it—not a fragment of any of the beautiful purple and gold drapes that had decorated the room which had been Allie Lane's. The Jovians had removed every object while I lay on the floor, apparently dead. Abaris' ray could not have struck me squarely, or else he had been too feeble and weak as the result of his wounds, to do more than stun me temporarily. In my rapid search of the room I discovered that the upheaval caused by the departure of the great interplanetary traveler, had sealed the tunnel in which I had hidden during the conflict between Sands and Abaris. The tunnel through which Abaris had suddenly appeared was likewise closed with massive rocks.

"As a last resort to escape from the underground world I began to study the possibility of crawling to the surface of the Manalava Plain through the wide fissure overhead. The opening was too high for me to reach up and obtain enough of a handhold to support my weight. I spent hours, working constantly, piling some of the broken rocks from the tunnels under the fissure. Eventually I succeeded in grasping a sharp rock protruding from the side of the crevice and hoisted myself up. It was hard, that climb to the outer world.

"Presently after what seemed hours of back-breaking labor I reached the surface. How good it was to breathe the pure air of Death Valley again! The atmosphere, in spite of the terrific heat of the Manalava Plain, was sweet glowing overhead. So entranced were Professor Bloch and I as he told it, that we failed to notice that the shrouds of night were lifting in the east as the sun cast its first vermilion rays into the darkened heavens.

Through the night the foreman had continued his tale uninterrupted and when he eventually finished, mumbling his thanks to us, the desert world had suddenly become brilliant with the everchanging colors of a desert dawn. I stared intently into the glowing coals of the camp fire, fascinated over the strange experiences he had unfolded to us. It was hard, very hard, to believe that tale, but somehow, it rang true. I shuddered at the thought of the grotesque Jovians and their uncanny powers.

The Professor remained silent lost in deep thought, apparently mulling over the story in his scientific way. I glanced at him quickly, expecting to see doubt written plainly on his features. Instead they were more serious than I had ever beheld them. The foreman hung his head in a stupor of exhaustion.

"Dowell!" Professor Bloch suddenly called to me as I sat staring into the fire. The abruptness of his voice caused me to jump nervously.

"Yes, Professor," I answered, very glad that the awesome silence which had settled over us after the foreman had finished his narrative, had been broken. "I'm very much awake sir."

"My friend," said the Professor, seriously, "you have heard this gentleman's weird story. Tell me plainly just how you have taken it. Do not be afraid to express yourself."

and beautiful. My lungs, long since taxed with the foul, nauseating atmosphere of the tunnels and caverns deep below me, pumped madly, as I breathed in the delightful air of my own world!

"The Manalava Plain as far as I could see had strangely become ruffled and strewn with broken rocks. Wide fissures and crevices were visible at every hand and on several occasions as I picked my way off the Plain I was forced to leap over them or make wide detours in order to pass. After terrible torture I eventually reached the spring in the little hidden canyon. There I drank deeply of the water that had previously been pale green in color and was now strangely colorless. I looked around the weather-broken wagons and searched the old trunk that Sands had found before we started to follow the phantom wagon with its two mysterious humans, but failed to find anything in which I could carry a supply of water. After rolling in the spring I struck off across the Valley. It was hell, friends, and I would have lain down many times to die, but the ever present vision of my wife and youngsters over at Balch, constantly beckoned me to continue. So here I am and I thank you, gentlemen, for saving my life!"

IX

I Have Doubts

THUS ENDED THE STRANGEST and most fascinating narrative that I had ever heard in my entire career as a newspaperman. I sat breathless at the very fearlessness with which the man narrated it and I could not help but believe him. It seemed impossible for him to conjure in his imagination, in so short a time, such a weird story. It could not have been done even by the most versatile tellers of fabricated stories!

Long before he had finished his narrative, night had fallen and with it had come its myriads of brilliant stars

"Well, Professor," I said, nervously. "It is difficult for a layman to accept such a story without basic facts, yet I feel that certain portions of it are true. Taking into consideration the fact that astronomers have just about proven that life exists on certain distant planets, it is not difficult to believe their assertions that its development there could be much further advanced than our own in scientific achievements. It seems quite natural that any form of life on Jupiter would differ greatly from our own due to atmospheric conditions and environment. As for radium, it seems quite possible that a great quantity of it would contain more qualities than are found in the small amounts of the metal that we have been able to obtain. However, in my opinion there seems to be but one factor in the narrative that has caused me to doubt a certain portion of it."

Pausing, I cast a quick glance at the mine-foreman. His head still hung in the stupor of exhaustion. He appeared to be sleeping soundly in a squatting position. I looked at Professor Bloch. He was regarding me thoughtfully, chin resting on his sun-tanned fists. Then I continued:

"It seems to me, Professor," I said, eyeing him, "that if the Jovians were immortal and could not be killed as this gentleman has related, there could be no existing skeletal remains. You say that Dr. Jamesson has recovered a huge skull. This man claims it fits perfectly with the facial characteristics of the Jovians. Under those conditions it is hard to accept that part of the narrative due to the fact that this man says that the Jovians cannot be destroyed and yet identifies a skull as being in exact conformity with the cranial structure of the terrestrial beings. How could it be possible to recover the skeletal remains of any creature that is allegedly immortal and therefore immune to death?"

"Your scientific observations and opinions, my friend," Professor Bloch said, enthusiastically, "are great for a newspaperman! I congratulate you! Your City Editor told me that you were the best hand on the *Outstander* at scientific matters and I believe him. However, I have gone over the narrative thoroughly and find in it the very same faults you have mentioned. But I actually believe this man told the truth! The green tint which marks his skin was undoubtedly caused by radium. I have seen radium affliction several times and its power discolors the human skin permanently when it is exposed to its rays for any length of time. I agree with you when you say that radium in large quantities must have more qualities than are known to exist in the small amounts recovered.

"As for the huge skull which Dr. Jamesson recovered. It is my opinion that the Jovians were not entirely immortal—that is, when they are outside of their accustomed atmospheric conditions. It is easy to believe that they achieved immortality on their own planet, for we today, on this globe, are slowly approaching a period when longevity will be increased to an astonishing degree. It is my prediction that we, too, will some day have achieved immortality to a certain degree inasmuch as radium is already known to have removed the cancerous tissues of the human anatomy that cause death.

"However, I have reasons to believe that some of the Jovians were destroyed by the peculiar atmosphere of this earth when they arrived here. Naturally they could not be accustomed to our atmospheric conditions and results were that only the fittest survived the rigors of an alien planet. We must consider that years must have been consumed before they actually succeeded in locating the underground source of the radium deposit. Those who were unable to keep up the strenuous pace, weighted down by the earth's own atmosphere, were quite naturally cast aside. Some of them could not survive. Hence the skeletal remains recovered by Dr. Jamesson!"

"But, Professor," I argued, seriously, "How could they survive the slugs from this gentleman's gun? Such a slug as shot from his calibre of gun would kill an elephant instantly."

"That, my friend, is one of their secrets of immortality. I do not know how they could survive. I can merely hazard an opinion. This man narrated that a peculiar green liquid poured from the wounds. I am convinced, then, that a radium compound instead of blood, coursed through their veins with power enough to heal even the most gaping wounds instantly. Radium flowing through their anatomies would have the power to banish the leaden slugs even as they entered. The lead, like other lesser metals, would vanish into invisible atoms under the embrace of radium and would therefore have no more effect upon the Jovians than would pulverized dust. But great heat, alien atmospheric conditions or some tremendous violence, would actually destroy a Jovian if he were not of the most hardy sort. I feel certain of that, my friend!"

We remained all that day at the camp by the Mesquite Springs. After a hurried breakfast we lay down and slept until late afternoon. The heat was terrific and it beat down upon me with deadening effect. I slept through it, dreaming terrible dreams. Eventually I was awakened by Professor Bloch who had already prepared a light lunch. The mine-foreman was holding a pan of sizzling bacon over a tiny fire while the Professor set other victuals on the tail of the buckboard. I rubbed my eyes sleepily and tilted my hat forward to keep the burning sun from searing my face.

"We almost left you, Dowell." Professor Bloch laughed, good naturedly. "You were sleeping so sound and dreaming so pleasantly that I hated to disturb you, but our friend here thought it best to take you along."

"I'd just as soon die from the heat there, I guess, as melt completely here. Let's eat! I want to get back to Los Angeles. The City Editor is reserving a room for me in the ice-house!"

"Very well, we're starting now."

Immediately after lunch we started across the Valley toward the mysterious red streak of table-land that marked the Manalava Plain. For hours we rode in the bouncing buckboard—for hours, it seemed, we walked along side of it to relieve the laboring animals. The sun beat down with terrific intensity and the heat waves danced blindingly from the sand.

Eventually we found it necessary to continue on foot, leaving the burros and the buckboard in a little, partly sheltered arroyo. About noon we arrived at what the foreman claimed to be the spot where he and Sands had located the radium pool. The surface of the Manalava Plain was a jumble of broken rocks and a maze of wide crevices. We stared at a deep crater-like depression before us but it was void of anything in the form of liquid. Nothing but boulders lay in its basin and the sides had crumbled in steep, loose rock-slides!

For what seemed ages, we searched around the surface for some opening that might lead us down into the deserted tunnels and chambers of the Jovians. None could be found. Evidence of some great, recent upheaval was everywhere and search as we did we could locate no avenue by which we might enter the strange underground world.

Presently Professor Bloch decided that the underground domain had been destroyed completely by the upheaval, caused no doubt, by the tremendous force of the radium in propelling the space-traveler from this earth. Disconsolately we trailed back to the buckboard.

When we eventually returned to Los Angeles, Professor Bloch refused to make a public statement regarding the foreman's strange experiences, and I was henceforth unable to submit the narrative for publication in the *Outstander*. I did, however, write an account of Dr. Jamesson's discovery of the peculiar skull and hinted indirectly at its remote connection with the chain of evolution on this globe, and the possibility of this world being invaded at some future period by Martians, Jovians or Venusians, but the *Outstander* published only a few garbled paragraphs that were unintelligible and valueless.

One thing Professor Bloch did say was that if money and inventive skill could be obtained an attempt might be made to go to Jupiter to rescue the unfortunate trio. If such a thing were to happen I will be one of the crew.

The Phantom of Terror

I

The Phantom

PROFESSOR JEROME MORTENSON, hunched over the work bench in his private laboratory, looked around suspiciously at the sound of stealthy feet behind him, and found himself looking into the cold, unwavering muzzle of an automatic. The masked, midnight intruder who held the weapon in a steady hand, halted abruptly in his tracks and crouched tensely. He breathed hard, making the only sounds audible in the instrument-filled room.

"Stand up, professor!" the intruder said coldly. "Don't try anything!"

Mortenson eyed the man calmly from head to foot, his gray, penetrating eyes trying hard to see behind the polka-dotted 'kerchief that hid the fellow's features from the bridge of his nose downward. All that he saw, however, were a pair of beady eyes, flashing with deadly earnest, a muscular figure that filled a well-cut brown suit, polished black oxfords and a white flannel cap, the latter pulled rakishly down over the right temple. The man's eyes fascinated him for a moment. A devilish light seemed to radiate from them with almost stunning force. They gave him the aspect of a dangerous man.

"What do you want?" Mortenson grumbled, appraising him.

The intruder chuckled softly, never once removing his steady gaze from the apprehensive features of his victim. He fumbled into a side pocket of his coat and brought out a scrap of wrinkled newspaper which he handed to the scientist with an insolent shrug.

"You should have had better sense, professor," he said coldly, "than to tell the world that you had discovered a way to penetrate and enter the Fifth Dimension!"

Mortenson reached out for the paper, a startled look in his eyes now. His hand trembled suddenly as he unfolded the clipping and glanced over it.

"I presume you refer to my interview with the editor of the *Journal?*" he inquired, controlling his anger and fear. "What has that to do with you?"

"Plenty!" the fellow snapped, advancing a step. "I want the apparatus you used to enter the Fifth Dimension!"

that he would be doing the law-abiding citizenry a great favor by meekly writing out instructions as to how to operate the fifth dimensional apparatus. The daring crook would undoubtedly meet his just deserts, if he ventured behind the veil into the mysterious world of the fifth dimension. The law of man would not be required, he thought, to bring the man to justice. What lay beyond would see to that.

He shivered a trifle as he thought of it. Swiftly his fingers flew over the typewriter. Meanwhile the crook stood over him, glaring hostilely, his gun in readiness to send instant death into the man whose life had been spent delving into the mysteries of the dimensions. The ignorant fellow could not know what was in store for him, and he had refused to listen to cold reason. Mortenson's warning had come from the heart. He had seen what lay behind the veil, and had been so sick and nauseated at what he saw, that he had slept little for some nights thereafter. But let the obstinate fellow go.

Mortenson yanked a sheet of paper from his typewriter, glancing over it quickly and stood erect.

"There you are, my friend," he said with a shrug. "The instructions are full and complete. I'll get the apparatus for you."

"Mortenson," the man snapped coldly. "If you've bunked me I'll come back and blast you into hell! Get that?"

"Never fear, young man," the scientist said, eyeing the fellow squarely. "The instructions are perfect and simple. Follow them to your doom. Now for the apparatus . . ."

"You must be crazy," Mortenson gasped weakly. "You could never make use of it!"

The intruder grunted and Mortenson heard the click of the safety catch as the man's thumb slid along the side of his automatic.

"That's where you come in!" he said curtly. "You're going to see that I *can* make use of it."

"What do you mean?" the scientist asked innocently.

"You know what I mean!" the man hissed sharply. "Don't try to pull that *innocent* stuff on me. You're going to hand over your Fifth Dimensional apparatus with instructions on how to use it. Now hop!"

"You don't know what you're doing," Mortenson argued desperately. "You must be insane!"

"Don't I?" the man jeered. "What do you think I came here for?"

"The apparatus, of course," said Mortenson, glancing about him furtively in search of a handy hammer or a weapon, "but, good Lord, man, you must be fond of trouble!"

"I'm used to it!" the intruder snarled. "And I'm giving you two minutes to hand it over!"

"That interview did not tell what actually exists in the Fifth Dimension," the scientist said dryly. "It's a terrible, invisible world filled with strange beasts that would tear a man to pieces, should he be caught there."

"You're a calm liar, professor!" the other jeered venomously. "It says plainly that the Fifth Dimension is nothing more than a curtain of invisibility!"

"Of course," Mortenson replied evenly. "I said that, because I did not want to frighten narrow-minded people with the knowledge that on every side lurk weird, ferocious man-beasts that would annihilate them, were it possible for them to emerge from behind the veil that hides the Fifth Dimension from human vision."

The intruder glared at him, his eyes narrowed suspiciously. Then he shrugged his broad shoulders decisively.

"You've got one more minute to deliver the goods, professor!" he barked. "I want the apparatus and instructions on how to operate it. Now sit down at your typewriter and pound 'em out!"

"It's all right with me, young fellow," said Mortenson resignedly, "if you want to seal your own doom. That's what you are going to do if you do some criminal act and place yourself in the Fifth Dimension to escape apprehension. It's your life, not mine. You won't listen to reason. I hate to see it. . . . "

"Shut up!" the other growled. "Sit down and write fast!"

"If I should refuse?" Mortenson paused at his typewriter.

"Then I'll drill you," the intruder snapped, tensing.

Mortenson hadn't a qualm of doubt but that the fellow would kill him in cold blood if he refused. And Mortenson had a great desire to live. He had just discovered a way to penetrate, neutralize and enter the invisible world of the Fifth Dimension. He was on the verge of doing great things in the world of science, and he had no intentions of removing himself from it by refusing the demands of this daring crook who was, doubtless as dangerous as he was fearless.

As he sat down at the typewriter he had a sudden feeling

"Just a minute, professor," the crook cut in. "You got any plans for the apparatus?"

Mortenson glanced at him shrewdly, suspiciously. He shook his head.

"No, I have not," he lied glibly. "I have no way of duplicating the apparatus, if that's what you mean."

"That's it exactly," the other sneered. "If you're lying—"

"I'm not!" the scientist grumbled. "I have not yet had time to make plans or illustrations. Not getting cold feet, are you?"

The man laughed peculiarly.

"Do I look yellow?" he grunted.

Mortenson agreed silently that he certainly did not look like a coward. But maybe the yellow streak would show up afterward, when it was too late to save himself. He smiled grimly and turned his back on the man. Quickly he strode to a big steel vault that stood in one corner of the room. The doors hung open. He bent over and removed a strange-looking helmet and an oval apparatus to which was attached a wide metal belt. Wires ran down from the helmet and hung loosely with small plugs dangling at the ends. In front of the helmet were firmly attached two projecting tubes. With the helmet in place on a man's head, these tubes fitted in front of the eyes, like field glasses.

The crook appraised the apparatus calmly. He displayed not a trace of excitement now, but Mortenson's blood pounded at his temples. He did not object to handing over his instruments, if they were to cause justice to place the hand of doom on the man who was robbing him and who had and would rob others. Within ten days he could construct other sets. The plans were in a safe-deposit vault in the bank. Mortenson was nobody's fool, though it had not entered his mind when he gave the *Journal* editor the interview, that his inventions would ever fall into the hands of the underworld. He was vaguely sorry now that he had allowed the news to be published, but it was too late for regret now. The thing was done.

"There you are, young fellow," he said, placing the apparatus in a heap on the bench. "Take it and be damned to you!"

"I didn't figure to get it so easy," the crook said, advancing toward the bench. "I've got a hunch you're trying to be smart!"

He glared at the scientist evilly, his fiery eyes glittering like the pink orbs of a snake.

"How do you put this stuff on?" he added with a snap.

"Helmet over the head, cylinders in front at the eyes," said Mortenson, hiding a grin. "Belt around the waist with attachment at the back. Plug the wires into the oval unit and send yourself into hell!"

"Funny, aren't you?" the fellow growled. "Is that all?"

"Wait and see!" Mortenson mused.

"If you're pulling a fast one . . . here! Take this to remember what'll happen to you if you are!"

The crook stepped forward suddenly. Before Mortenson had time to move the automatic crashed with a thud on his head. He sank to the floor with a groan, a terrible roar in his brain, great, dancing lights spinning before his dazed eyes. The intruder looked at him once, stepped over the still body and picked up the apparatus. With a pleased grin he made for the door and vanished into the night.

II

The Robbery

WHEN PROFESSOR JEROME MORTENSON regained his senses a midday sun was casting its brilliant light and warmth through a skylight directly over him. His head throbbed painfully, his lips were dry and feverish. Dark stains on his shirt-front made him feel his aching head. His hair was matted with coagulated blood, his cheek was caked. He marvelled that he had survived the terrible blow at all.

Half-dazed he stood up, swaying like a drunken man. The room spun like a top. He closed his eyes to steady himself, then lurched slowly toward a wash-stand to douse his head in cold water. A trickle of vermillion ran down his temple after the dried blood had been washed from a gaping scalp wound that would require atleast three stitches to close. Holding a towel over the gash he sat down to his telephone, called a doctor, and waited in gloomy silence for his arrival.

He did not have long to wait, however. Within fifteen minutes the medico was on the scene and in less time the wound was stitched and bandaged. Feeling the effects of a sedative administered to him, Mortenson became more alert. Rapidly his mind raced over the robbery. To make sure that he was not dreaming he went to his safe. The fifth dimensional apparatus was gone all right.

"Damn!" he ejaculated softly, and then: "Oh, well! It's a wonder the devil didn't kill me. He thought I was fooling with him, but . . . "

The shrill cry of a newsboy outside suddenly attracted his attention. He listened as the cries grew louder. Trembling he went to the door and stepped out into the open. The sun was dazzling and made his head ache violently for a moment. The newsy paused in the street and yelled at him.

"Paper, mister?" he cried sharply. "Extra! All about the phantom bandit!"

Mortenson dug into his pocket and bought a paper. The headlines made him wince. Quickly he returned to his laboratory, sat down and began reading with a strange feeling of helplessness.

Like a colorful character stepping out of a fantastic Edgar Allen Poe story, a lone bandit early today held up the Farmers' National Bank here, shot and killed James Sprowl, a teller, and escaped with approximately $250,000.00 in cash.

The holdup occurred shortly after the bank opened its doors this morning and according to Martin Jones, Sprowl's assistant, employees were forced to line up beside the vault at the command of a man who appeared as if by magic.

Speaking almost hysterically of the bold daylight robbery, Jones is quoted as saying:

"The bandit seemed to appear out of thin air and wore a strange mask that had two long cylindrical objects sticking out from the eyes. He had not been seen to enter the bank after the doors were opened.

"I heard his command, even before I could see anything more than a vague shadow looming up in front of our cage, and then there appeared a peculiar glow around it from which emerged the bandit.

"He covered Sprowl and me first. I do not recall just what happened and I'm not certain if Sprowl grabbed the gun under the counter. But the mysterious bandit's automatic exploded and Sprowl fell dead at my feet.

"With everyone cowed and appalled, the man forced us to fill a bag with all available cash and with the money he vanished into the air again right before our eyes. For a full minute, thereafter, there was a peculiar blue haze in the spot where he vanished. I heard him laugh weirdly as he disappeared like a ghost."

Mortenson continued to read the accounts for some minutes; then suddenly he was interrupted by a loud knock on the door. He jumped nervously, laid the paper aside and went to it. He hand shook on the knob and his lips twitched. He swung the door wide open, to find himself confronted by two burly detectives. They displayed their badges with little formality. But Mortenson knew what they were after.

"Come right in, gentlemen," he invited quickly. "I've been expecting this call."

"Oh, you have, eh?" Detective-Lieutenant Barton grunted sarcastically. He glanced over Mortenson with shrewd, suspicious eyes and entered. Riley, his companion, followed him, his right hand buried in his coat pocket. Barton continued: "What made you expect this call?" he snapped bluntly.

At first glance at the newspaper headlines, Mortenson knew he would be suspected of being the phantom bandit. The world already knew that he, of all people in it, had been the first man to solve the mysteries of the fifth dimension through the use of strange apparatus such as worn by the bandit, but he had little doubt of establishing his innocence, so far as the robbery and killing was concerned. He sat down heavily in a chair as though to prepare himself for an ordeal of questioning.

"Well," he said slowly, "having invented the apparatus used by the bandit to make himself invisible, and being known as the inventor, I would naturally expect to be questioned by the law, considering the circumstances under which that apparatus has been used. I presume I am suspected of being the phantom bandit?"

Barton scowled as though taken aback by the scientist's cool, straightforward speech. He glanced at Riley, whose steel-blue eyes twinkled with suspicion and amusement.

"You are not only suspected, but accused, Mortenson!" Barton growled. "What have you to say to that?"

The scientist appraised him calmly, a flush of warm blood mounting to his cheeks. His head throbbed again and made him slightly dizzy.

"I'll say that I can put you on the right track if you'll listen and don't go off half-cocked," he said curtly, beginning to resent the officer's hostile attitude.

"I suppose you'll deny your guilt?" Riley put in ruthlessly.

"I'd be a fool to confess to something I did not do," Mortenson informed him quickly. "You fellows seem pretty sure of yourselves, don't you?"

"Now, Mortenson," said Barton, shoving a cigar between his teeth and pausing to chew at it. "I don't want any beating about the bush. I want you to tell me exactly where you were this morning at nine-fifteen."

"That's easy, Barton," said Mortenson cooly. "I was lying right there on the floor, knocked out completely. As usual I worked late last night. About midnight a masked man came in here, robbed me of my fifth dimensional apparatus, knocked me cold with his gun and skipped. That's the reason for the bandages on my head and the cause for that blood-stain on the floor near your feet. I came too about an hour ago, had Doctor Brandon sew me up, and then bought a newspaper which informed me of the bank holdup and killing.

"I hardly blame you for suspecting me, but you can see at a glance that I had nothing to do with the bank affair, except, of course, giving the crook instructions as to how to operate the apparatus,"

"Why did you do that?" snapped Barton.

"To live, Barton," the scientist retorted. "You probably know what it is to face a gun, not knowing what minute it might go off."

The detectives exchanged baffled glances and Barton bent over to appraise the blood-stain on the floor. Riley's eyes roved about the room and finally concentrated on Mortenson's bandaged head.

"Suppose we have a look at that head, Mortenson," he said with a shrug of his powerful shoulders. Barton looked up.

"Never mind that, Riley," he said authoritively. "Let Wagner do that at headquarters."

"You mean you are going to take me in on suspicion?" Mortenson sat bolt upright.

"I've got a warrant for your arrest, Mortenson," the other replied firmly. "Your story sounds pretty good to me, but I'll have to book you at least. You'll probably be released on your own recognizance, if the police surgeon's report is satisfactory. You know . . . "

"Oh, I know, Barton," said the scientist with a nod. "You think I might have put that stain there and bashed my own head to establish an alibi. Well, you're all wrong. Look in the wash-stand and you will see that I washed the blood off my head and face there. It takes at least eight hours for blood to coagulate and I'm sure you will find clots in the sink to prove that I was injured shortly after midnight."

"Why didn't you report to headquarters when you came too?" Riley grumbled.

"I don't know," said Mortenson. "I guess I was too dazed. Then Dr. Brandon came and fixed me up. After that I became interested in the news of the bank robbery."

III

Mortenson Explains

ENTANGLED IN THE NET OF the law, Mortenson, despite his high social standing and fame as a scientist, was taken to police headquarters and summarily booked on suspicion. He went through the process of being finger-printed and "mugged" like a man in a trance. All the while his head ached violently, sending sharp, stabbing pains through his brain. The reaction of the blow was telling on him now and his hands shook. But he submitted to the rigid rules of the police department without protest, for he had little fear of failure in proving his innocence, if given the chance.

Finally Police Surgeon Wagner removed the bandage from his head and appraised the scientist's scalp. Already the edges of the gash were beginning to heal. A soft scab was forming at the ends of the cut.

"Lucky for you, Mortenson," Wagner said with a grin as he began to re-bandage the scientist's head, "that you have a thick skull. The blow might have killed a man less fortunate."

Mortenson nodded. "The devil hit me without warning," he mumbled, "with the barrel of his gun. Barton hinted that I bashed my head in to establish an alibi!"

"You'd have to be a contortionist to do that," laughed Wagner. "I get a huge kick out of some of the flat-feet we have on the detective force. You've been slugged and no mistake, Mortenson."

"Thanks, Wagner," said Mortenson warmly. "Doubtless you'll put that in your report."

"Of course," the surgeon replied, ripping some adhesive tape from a roll. "I couldn't do anything else in this case."

"Then I'll be turned loose," said Mortenson grimly, "on my own recognizance. If I can get help from the Police Department, I'll make it mighty hot for a certain bank robber . . . that is, if he hasn't already jumped into the fire. Time alone will tell."

Mortenson could not know that at that very moment the Phantom Bandit was again making his appearance in the heart of the city's banking district. This time the daring crook chose the Inter-State Bank for the scene of his activities. But as the scientist sat in Wagner's office waiting for the final cessation of police procedure, he heard the flying squad suddenly tear out of the adjoining station amid a riot of screaming sirens.

He could not help but conclude that something serious was taking place somewhere in the city. The scream of the sirens gradually subsided as the speeding police cars put distance between them and headquarters. Mortenson glanced at the surgeon as the telephone on his desk jingled. Wagner pressed a button quickly and the ambulance roared out of the receiving hospital driveway. The surgeon then glanced at Mortenson.

"The vanishing bandit robbed the Inter-State Bank, Mortenson," he said crisply. "Killed a watchman and shot up another teller. I guess that lets you out entirely, old man. You couldn't be the Phantom Bandit and a *fish* at the same time."

"Fish?" Mortenson queried blankly. "What do you mean?"

Wagner. laughed at the other's questioning expression. "Fish," he said quickly, "is what we call prisoners."

"Oh," mused Mortenson. "Teller hurt bad?"

"Dunno!" said Wagner. "They usually are when they're sent here." He turned to the officer into whose custody Mortenson had been placed for his visit to the receiving room. "Take Mr. Mortenson to the desk, Tully," said Wagner. "They'll want to release him and apologize. That's all! And good luck, Mortenson. Hope you catch the phantom bandit."

"Much obliged, Wagner," the scientist replied, rising. "I trust you'll be ready to receive his corpse."

Wagner chuckled. "In that case, send it next door," he

Steckel was astounded as he grasped the magnitude of the facts. He pressed the scientist for more information and got it.

"You see, chief," Mortenson said finally, "our visionary organs behold only the colors of the spectrum. Below and above each individual color is a deeper shade which our eyes cannot perceive because of the high or low vibrations of light, whichever the case may be. Now the Fifth Dimension lies above the violet shade. Physical science calls this 'color' the ultra-violet. It is a vast, invisible realm in itself, as invisible to us as our own world is to the creatures who inhabit the Fifth Dimension. It is invisible because of the rapid vibratory oscillation of its light scale. Color or rather ether waves have high light scales of vibration, too rapid or too slow to be perceived by the naked human eye. On each of these scales lie vast realms, some teeming with life of primitive or advanced state, others absolutely blank because of adverse electronic conditions.

"Taking the scale of light offered by the ultra-violet as my field of study and experiment, I succeeded in neutralizing the veil of invisibility, that enshrouds the Fifth Dimension. In doing this I overcome the vibrations of light and electrical current. By applying these oscillations to the physical body through the instrument I devised, and which, incidentally, was stolen from me last night, I was able to transfer my own body from our world to the realm of the Fifth Dimension. These vibrations and electronic movements, when applied to the physical body, cause it to become invisible at once and automatically transfer it to the particular scale to which they are aligned.

grinned. "The morgue handles the remains. Think you'll catch him?"

The surgeon's attention was diverted by a sudden screech of brakes outside. He gave Mortenson a passing glance and went out. Officer Tully escorted the scientist to the desk-sargeant.

"Heard the news, Mortenson?" the sergeant inquired, grinning.

"About the new robbery—phantom bandit?" the scientist grunted.

The sergeant nodded. "Robbed the Inter-State Bank in broad daylight and got away like a ghost," he responded talkatively. "By the way, what kind of an outfit was that he got from you?"

"Rather complicated to explain here, sergeant," Mortenson said, impatient to obtain his release.

"Yeah?" the other replied slowly. "One of those things, huh?"

"One of those things, sergeant," Mortenson repeated restlessly. "I suppose now the law is convinced that I am not the phantom bandit. If that is the case, I'd like to get back to work."

"Right you are, professor," the sergeant boomed. "Moreover, the chief requested a moment ago to have your fingerprints, picture and all personal records destroyed. He wants to have a talk with you, if you don't mind."

Mortenson's features brightened. "Of course," he nodded. "I wanted to talk with him. How soon can I see him?"

"Right away, sir!" the sergeant stated, turning to Tully

who had wandered off. "Tully!"—he called aloud. The
officer came up quickly. "Take Mr. Mortenson up to the
chief's office. He's waiting!"

Newspapermen thronged the office of Chief of Police
Steckel. Mortenson was mobbed until the chief interfered
with the eager reporters and ordered them to the press
room. The scientist had a keen dislike for notoriety and
displayed it at the onset by refusing to answer any of the
questions put to him by the zealous reporters. Chief Steckel,
seeing this, went immediately to his rescue. The office was
cleared quickly. Mortenson was invited to a chair.

"Professor Mortenson," the executive began without hesitation, "just what is the apparatus you report was stolen
from you, presumably by this so-called phantom bandit?"

The scientist settled back in his chair, frowning.

"I'm afraid you would not understand, chief," he said
complacently, "as it is very complicated. But if you like,
I'll explain it just as simply as I can."

Steckel shook his head eagerly, handed a cigar to the
scientist and lit one himself. Immersed in a cloud of blue,
fragrant smoke, Mortenson explained the principle of his
invention, its use to science and, unfortunately, to crime.
He told what lay behind the veil of the Fifth Dimension,
that invisible world beyond the vision of man, yet which
existed on every human hand; there in the office, up on the
roof and out on the streets. He went further to say that
even within the world of the Fifth Dimension others existed
—the Sixth, the Seventh and so on probably without limit!

But of them all, Mortenson had succeeded in neutralizing the curtain, behind which existed the Fifth Dimension.

"By adapting certain prismatic lenses to my eyes, I was able to visit and to perceive this ultra-violet world and all that exists in it within range of vision. You can imagine my amazement when I beheld a world of solids, that was tinted with a pale violet shade, as the earth is with gold at times of sunset. And my apparatus had placed me right in the midst of death and destruction! The Fifth Dimension teems with primitive life; is inhabited by strange creatures, armed with primitive but deadly weapons.

"That was my first venture into the realm of the Fifth Dimension, my dear Chief. And in my horror and fear I transferred myself back to our own world before the creatures recovered sufficiently from their surprise at seeing me to attack. I was afraid to venture there again, alone, and was working on a new form of weapon for defense, when I was held up and robbed of the instrument that made my visit to the ultra-violet realm possible. This phantom bandit is undoubtedly the very man who stole my apparatus, but for the life of me, I cannot understand how he manages to enter the Fifth Dimension and remain for any length of time, without being destroyed by the creatures who live there!"

Chief Steckel eyed him strangely, perhaps a trifle incredulous in his expression.

"You really mean then, Mortenson," he said softly and in a baffled tone, "that this vanishing killer-bandit can rob and murder and hide behind a curtain of invisibility beyond the reach of the law?"

"That gives us exactly his reason for taking my apparatus," said the scientist, "and obviously for what he is doing now, hiding somewhere in the Fifth Dimension, safe from human apprehension!"

"Good Lord, man!" Steckel exploded suddenly. "Does that mean we'll never have a chance to grab him?"

Professor Mortenson smiled shrewdly. "You'll never lay hands on him, Steckel," he said flatly. "Unless you give me your aid in carrying out a plan I have already devised. Even then it may be impossible, but we can try. Meanwhile this criminal is going to go about his way killing and robbing at will and may, at this very moment, be in this room!"

Steckel's face paled and his eyes flashed. Mechanically he glanced around as though searching for some imaginary eavesdropper. But Mortenson quickly placed him at ease.

"He could not hear a thing from this world if he is hiding in the other," he said. "Sound is similar to light in that respect. There are sounds too high or too low in pitch to be heard by our limited auditory capacities. The desperado would have to be right here and visible to hear what we say. He may watch every move I make now, for he warned me that I would be a dead man, the first attempt I made to follow him into the Fifth Dimension.

Steckel's eyes continued to flash apprehensively. "Why, the devil might have designs on *my* life," he said. "He might pop up at any moment, kill me for the good of the underworld, and vanish again! Or he might kill you if he thought you could duplicate the apparatus!"

Mortenson scrutinized the chief thoughtfully.

"He doesn't, chief," he said seriously. "At least that is my impression. I told him I had no plans of the instrument; that I could not duplicate them. Had he believed otherwise, I'd have gotten his bullet instead of a crack on the skull."

"But you can duplicate them, Mortenson?" the chief asked eagerly.

Mortenson laughed shrewdly. "Of course," he replied. "I have a complete set of plans. I merely lied to save my neck!"

"You intend to use them, then?" Steckel inquired, leaning forward.

The scientist nodded. Without hesitation he explained his scheme. Steckel listened intently, his eyes narrowed.

"So you see," Mortenson finally concluded, "we can make it mighty hot for the killer if I get the support of your department. It will be an exceptionally dangerous adventure, but worth . . . "

"Then count me in personally!" Steckel injected quickly. "If we can lay our hands on the phantom bandit by going into the Fifth Dimension after him, it will be worth the chance we take. When you are ready I'll detail eight men to your services. Moreover, the department will stand the expense of duplicating your apparatus . . . ten complete sets. I think it would be well to start immediately, don't you?"

"Right!" ejaculated Mortenson, rising. "But it will take ten days or more to build the instruments."

Steckel groaned. "Meanwhile the crook will keep on operating!" he said grimly. "The city will be at his mercy until the sets are finished. But I guess it can't be helped."

"No," said the scientist slowly, "it can't be helped."

IV

The Visitor

DAYS PASSED SWIFTLY. GOLD seemed to have become an obsession with the phantom bandit. The police were powerless. The crook robbed and killed at will, feeling safe and secure in his ability to swoop down and vanish, leaving the alert minions of the law baffled completely. In three days he had robbed four banks and escaped with his loot. He left death and fear behind him on each occasion. Then for a whole day he failed to appear, but Mortenson felt that he would return. And he did, the following day, to loot the city treasury of a quarter million dollars! ·

Then the rumbling of public protest echoed through the press. Chief Steckel and his department were at once swamped in a vortex of caustic sentiment. But the chief had been under fire before and remained silent, while the press made light of his ability to cope with the underworld forces, particularly with the phantom bandit. He was powerless and knew it, yet he kept secret his negotiations with Professor Mortenson. It would never do to allow that to get out! Before Mortenson could complete his apparatus, the phantom crook would swoop down upon him and kill him. What then? Chief Steckel was no fool, and he took the bitter dose without complaint.

The *"Journal"* boldly asked the mayor and the police commission to dismiss him. Steckel was called on the carpet and thoroughly denounced. Sentiment and unmerciful nagging were beginning to disrupt the whole department, a fine machine that he had built up for the protection of the people. He smiled grimly through it all, and finally asked for a fifteen day stay of removal. This was granted to him by the mayor despite the protests of the press and the commission. Steckel laughed secretly and told himself that there'd be a change of opinion at the end of fifteen days.

Meanwhile, Mortenson, with five expert opticians and three master mechanics under him, worked doggedly in his laboratory. The laboratory adjoined the scientist's big house where they consumed their meals hurriedly. Mortenson slept with the men a few hours each night in the workroom. Plain-clothes men lurked about the place as a precaution against a raid on the scientist by the vanishing criminal who, they suspicioned, might have learned through the grapevine system what was going on.

But the crook appeared to have taken Mortenson's word that it was impossible to duplicate the instrument that transferred him from one plane to another. He seemed satisfied to add to his already fabulous coffers and let the scientist alone. Perhaps he was afraid of Mortenson, fearing that the scientist might have evolved some means of nullifying the effect of the vibration on the physical body.

Mortenson was elated at his progress, but he had a constant fear of the criminal. Doubtlessly the man would kill him if he learned that he was putting his heart and soul into the work of building sufficient apparatus to outfit a squad of police officers who would use them to hunt him down in the mysterious, invisible world. Yet the scientist worked dauntlessly, night and day, feeling more secure with each passing hour as the instruments neared completion.

To kill Mortenson, the desperado would first have to emerge from behind the veil of the Fifth Dimension. To do this would lay him open for immediate death at the hands of the officers and plainclothes men, who constantly guarded the scientist. As a further precaution, Mortenson was on the alert at all times. He was armed and ready to defend his life, yet there persisted within him a constant fear that the man would unexpectedly appear and shoot him in the back.

Finally Mortenson stepped back and appraised ten complete Fifth Dimension sets neatly arranged on the workbench. Each set was equipped with a wide metal belt, attached to which was a small, oval box containing storage batteries capable of releasing vibratory electronic current. Loose wires as thin as thread, with small plugs at the ends, ran from the head-gear. The gear appeared like field glasses connected to a leather helmet. But inside the leather ran meshed wire with bare electrodes exposed to fit snugly against the forehead and the back of the neck.

He trembled with excitement when he realized that at last the job was completed. The plans had been followed to the minutest detail. Nothing could go wrong and Mortenson shivered at the thought of what lay behind the curtain that hid the Fifth Dimension from view. He meditated a moment on the miracle that had prevented the phantom terror from meeting his doom behind the veil. Then his telephone disrupted his thoughts. He went to it at once. His caller was Chief Steckel and his voice trembled fearfully.

"My God, Mortenson," he informed the scientist. "The phantom bandit shot at me on Broadway a few moments ago! His slug creased my shoulder!"

"No!" Mortenson was incredulous. "Why would he want to kill you?"

"I told you before, Mortenson," Steckel said, "that he might kill me for the benefit of the underworld! They couldn't buy me off for protection, but they could kill me to intimidate the Department!"

"You mean actually that the fellow shot at you right on Broadway?" Mortenson inquired dubiously.

"He did!" snapped Steckel. "What's more, he took a chunk out of my shoulder! Before he could shoot again a crowd surged around him. He vanished in a blue haze like a ghost!"

"It seems incredible that the fellow would be so bold," said Mortenson, "but will your wound interfere with your going into the other world?"

"I'm not hurt seriously enough for that," responded the chief. "How soon are you going to be ready?"

"Right away, Steckel," said the scientist grimly. "I was going to call you in a few moments. But get your squad and come on over to my laboratory. Everything is ready!"

"Good!" said Steckel. "Take my advice and watch your step! That fellow may try to get you! I think he's been tipped off to our plans!"

"Don't worry about me," said Mortenson lightly. "I'm well guarded."

The Chief hung up the receiver and turned to his staff of assistants. The work was completed and he needed them no longer. His payroll was already prepared and he paid them off. They were dismissed, but as they filed through the door, Mortenson kept his right hand in his pocket. His fingers closed tightly around the butt of an automatic. He was taking no chances on a sudden appearance of the phantom bandit.

For fully five minutes after the last man had gone out of the room, he stood beside the bench and waited silently. Then cautiously he went to the door and barred it from the inside. With a sigh of relief he turned. A blue haze appeared suddenly before him. It made him blink for an instant. Then out the shimmering, vibrating mist appeared the form of a man.

Had Professor Mortenson been struck by lightning, he could have been no more stunned or electrified. He recoiled, throwing his arms up as though to shield his face from a blow. Out of the dimming haze emerged a man, looking grotesque in a Fifth Dimension helmet. In his right hand was a blunt-nosed automatic. Mortenson's face went bloodless.

The phantom bandit stood before him, a cold, significant sneer on his lips. Suddenly he laughed outright, like a man without a soul. The tone of it filled Mortenson with a deep-seated fear.

"You—you've come back!" he gasped, glancing about him wildly.

The bandit laughed again in a weird display of mirth. Something had changed the man, re-made him entirely, Mortenson thought. He was not the young, dashing desperado that had appeared in the laboratory ten days previously and walked away with the Fifth Dimensional apparatus! This man had a stubble of gray beard on his chin and his clothes were tattered and torn. And he seemed like a man who had gone through hell and left his soul with the devil's imps!

"I said I'd come back, didn't I, professor?" he snapped savagely. "I thought you were telling me the truth, the night I cracked you on the head. But you're a liar, Mortenson!"

"But . . ." Mortenson began, stammering.

"Shut up!" the bandit cut in with an oath. "You thought you could fool me, didn't you, Mortenson? But you didn't, know what I'm driving at. In case you don't, I'll enlighten you. I'd like to have a man like you on my side and I'm willing to pay a big price, too. I'm going to organize a bunch of my friends and declare the Fifth Dimension as my inviolate domain. In exchange for your services and help I'd make you my right hand man. With your brains and my guts, we could go a long way, but listen! I don't really need you! I can have those devices duplicated any-time! I'm merely giving you a chance to live. What do you say?"

Bribery! But why would this man try to tempt him? What could he, Mortenson, do that would aid the under-world, unless it was to build Fifth Dimensional apparatus to outfit the phantom criminal's followers?

Mortenson studied the man meditatively, his brain work-ing rapidly. So the fellow wanted his services, eh? Why, when he could have the apparatus duplicated by some cor-rupt scientist? Or could anyone duplicate them at all, be-yond himself? Mortenson's eyes narrowed as he grasped the full significance of the man's bold proposition.

The apparatus could not be duplicated by anyone but himself! That was why the bandit was so intent upon en-listing his aid to set up a domain of terror in the Fifth Dimension, a domain that would prey unmercifully upon the world in which he now stood. That was Mortenson's conclusion and it was correct. The bandit had tried else-where to have the apparatus duplicated and had failed. Without Mortenson's help his mad, daring scheme would also fail.

Mortenson stroked his chin in silence. His attitude was

you sneak! You never stopped to think that I'd have you watched, did you?"

Mortenson winced. His vitals seemed to turn over within him at the cold chill of the killer's now sharp, biting voice. He was getting control of himself rapidly now and he stood in the middle of the floor like a graven image. He could not see the man's eyes, for they were hidden behind the vision cylinders of the helmet. But he could watch the fellow's lips. They were thick and cruel and curled up to the right side of his mouth with almost every word he spoke.

"Then why didn't you kill me a week ago?" the scientist hissed suddenly.

Again the bandit laughed. "I just wanted to see how far you'd go, Mortenson!" he snarled. "I thought I'd let you get your ten sets of apparatus built and then bump you off for your trouble!"

"You're a cool liar!" said the scientist boldly. "There's something deeper than that. You thought you'd let me build ten more sets so you could take them for your pals, eh?"

"You astound me with your psychic powers, professor!" the bandit sneered. "Of course I wanted the other sets! But I'm going to kill you nevertheless! Isn't it a disappointment to have worked like a dog merely to be killed in the end?"

Mortenson was perfectly aware of that, but his deadly cold features failed to display the truth. He laughed loudly in the man's face.

"You're not going to kill me or anybody else, my friend!"

he said perhaps a trifle hysterically. "All I need to do it to call the guards!"

"Humph!" the killer growled. "I fixed every bull on the place; knocked every one of them cold. They're a bunch of lazy flat-feet!"

"Good Lord, man!" gasped Mortenson, sobering. "Don't tell me you killed all those detectives!"

"No, I didn't kill 'em!" the other barked. "But it'll be a month before they get over their headaches! Now listen to me, Mortenson. You're a damned smart man . . . " he lowered his voice, "and I hate to kill smart men . . . "

"You don't say!" Mortenson cut in sarcastically.

"Shut your mouth!" the bandit snarled, shoving forth his gun in a significant gesture. "I'll do the talking! You listen until I ask you to speak!"

The scientist, resolved that if he was destined to die, he would do so like a man and he realized suddenly that if ever a man faced death, he was facing it now. But somehow, after his first scare, he was not frightened and in a few moments Steckel would arrive with his squad. If he could stall the bandit along until then, well . . . .

The killer's voice diverted his thoughts.

"As I was saying," he said softly," you're a smart man and I understand you're not very well fixed financially. Now just supposing I'd settle a million on your bank account . . . just supposing I would. Would that make any difference in your life?"

"Just what do you mean, young man?" Mortenson arched his brows.

"Don't stall, professor!" the man ordered curtly. "You

that of a man deciding an important issue in deep thought. The bandit squinted at him shrewdly, a leering smile on his almost diabolical lips. Then Mortenson addressed him.

"What about the creatures in the Fifth Dimension?" he asked curtly.

Before the criminal could make a reply, there came the sound of heavy footsteps from the hall leading to the laboratory from the outside. Instantly the man tensed, jerking his automatic in line with the door. Mortenson's heart pounded like a triphammer. Chief Steckel and his men had arrived. But were they in time?

The phantom bandit backed slowly toward the work bench on which lay the ten completed sets of Fifth Dimension apparatus. A heavy knock rattled the laboratory door. The bandit squinted at the scientist.

"Well, what about it, Mortenson?" he hissed coldly. "You with me or not?"

The scientist winced as the man levelled his automatic at him.

"I haven't had time to decide," he replied in a quivering voice. He glanced at the door. It was barred, but through it he could hear the voices of the men outside.

"Then I'll be generous with you and give you twelve hours to make up your mind," he jeered. "Meantime I'm going to take care of these ten sets of apparatus."

A wave of fear and desperation went over Mortenson as he realized that the man was going to make away with the Fifth Dimensional devices. He felt an urge to cry out to Steckel to smash down the door, but the bandit's pistol prevented it. In his pocket lay his own automatic, but it was useless now. If he made one move to draw it the bandit would undoubtedly kill him without a qualm.

Suddenly he seemed to calm. He overcame a wild roving of his eyes and settled them on the bandit. Then slowly he advanced toward the man, speaking in a lowered voice. "You say there's a million in it for me?" he asked in a half whisper.

The bandit nodded and relaxed. "Yeah!" he said quickly. "And more if you play ball with me."

"How do I know you will not double-cross me?" Mortenson asked, advancing carelessly.

"When I give my word, I don't go back on it," the bandit replied with a perfunctory shrug. He lowered his automatic a trifle, impressed by the scientist's interest in his proposition.

"All right!" said Mortenson decisively. He halted within four feet of the bandit and jerked his thumb at the door. "Speak low," he said, "or they'll hear you. Now, it'll take twenty thousand to start building apparatus on a big scale."

"That's fine," the bandit nodded, pulling a roll of bills from a pocket and glancing at it carelessly. By sheer force of desperation, Mortenson lashed out savegly and brought both hands down on the man's gun-arm. Instantly the automatic spat like a whiplash and then clattered to the floor. With an oath he swung around at the scientist, his roll of bills scattering.

Screaming at the top of his voice, Mortenson lunged himself bodily at the phantom bandit. His arms caught him around the waist. They fell to the floor, Mortenson yelling at the officers outside.

"Steckel!" he screamed wildly. "Break down the door! BREAK IT DOWN!"

A savage foot caught Mortenson on the chest and sent him spinning. There was a rending crash of splintering wood and into the laboratory rushed Steckel and his men. Mortenson stared at them in a daze.

"Get him, Steckel!" he scrieked. "He's lying on the floor near the bench!"

Automatics drawn, the officers glanced toward the bench. Above it hovered a pale blue haze that shimmered like a curtain of smoke. From it came a venomous curse that all could hear before the phantom bandit vanished completely into the Fifth Dimension.

"I'll get you for that, Mortenson!" the bandit snarled. "You dirty double-crosser! I'll get you if it's the last . . ." His voice trailed off into nothing as he penetrated the veil between the two worlds.

"Did you hear that, Steckel?" Mortenson gasped, rising.

"What's it all about?" Steckel grumbled, mystified.

"The phantom bandit!" exclaimed the scientist. "He was in here . . you heard his voice! I tackled him in an effort to hold him, but he kicked me and got away."

Mortenson rushed to his work bench. On it lay the untouched apparatus. His mad lunge at the bandit and the appearance of the officers had thwarted the desperado's intentions of making away with them. The scientist gave a sigh of relief and turned to Steckel.

"Let's get started, chief," he said urgingly. "There's no time to lose. The bandit is somewhere close and we must catch him. My life isn't worth a counterfeit penny now!"

V

Into the Fifth Dimension

WITH CHIEF STECKEL AND eight grim-faced officers including Barton and Riley lined up, Mortenson hurridly gave instructions on the operation of the Fifth Dimensional apparatus. Each man wore a set, giving them the appearance of gargantuan creatures of another world, with the projecting eyes, tight-fitting helmets and wide metal belts. They looked like men from Mars, but Mortenson had no time to make such observations or any comparisons.

He had made some important improvements over the first

set of apparatus taken by the phantom bandit. The new ones were equipped with a small panel that hung down over the chest. On this were three buttons arranged in numerical order so that the wearer could press number one and start the electronic vibrations coursing gently through the body, and on down to number three which actually neutralized the veil of invisibility between the two worlds. This arrangement, he thought, made the apparatus fool-proof.

Finally the scientist donned his own set. As he swung the lenses before his eyes he glanced along the line of men. Each officers held an improved model sub-machine gun capable of firing a hundred rounds of ammunition at one loading. They were short, squat weapons with cartridge disks on the barrel just before the stock grip. A grim set of men, he concluded, who would stop at nothing to apprehend the desperado who struck without warning like a *fer de lance*, leaving death and terror on his invisible trail.

"Are you all ready, men?" Mortenson inquired suddenly. A murmur of assent ran along the line. "Remember what I told you . . . in event any of you are wounded in the world which we are now to enter and want to transfer yourself back here in a hurry, press all three buttons simultaneously. The vibratory reaction will probably knock you out for a moment, but it will not harm you. Take note of your surroundings when we enter the Fifth Dimension so that you can mark the spot for the return to this laboratory. Now, gentlemen, place your fingers on the control buttons and press number one. Allow a count of five seconds to pass, then press number two and repeat the operation until after number three has been pressed. Ready! Press number one!"

A faint throbbing surged through the ten men as they simultaneously pressed the first button. The laboratory went aglow with the pale blue luminosity. Then the throbbing intensified, whirring like the wings of a honeybee. To an observer the men might have appeared to vanish slowly from the room in a thin vapor of blue. The electronic current played around them in a shimmering curtain, the electrodes pressing against their flesh creating a slight burning sensation. Their muscles seemed to jerk as the vibrations intensified. As they pressed the third button the throbbing became a high-pitched whine, rising in tone until it almost screamed.

Each man felt a sinister dizziness as he left the laboratory. After a moment of nausea and the sensation of falling into an abysmal pit, they felt no other reaction to the rapid vibrations of the apparatus. But the current continued to whine, sending the oscillations throughout their bodies and weapons with unceasing force. Gradually the weird, spectral world of the Fifth Dimension unfolded itself before them. From their eye-instruments shot twin jets of violet light, that seemed to illuminate a jumbled mass before them. Slowly the terrain of the Fifth Dimension assumed definite shape. It was a rolling, uneven world, covered with a tall violet lush and spectral forests of deep blue. No tall mountains were visible; rather was the Fifth Dimension a place of undulating hills, rolling and rippling as far as they could see.

Just rimming the horizon stood a ball of violet flame. Mortenson knew it was the sun, but he was not certain if it was rising or setting. Its heat made them uncom-

Slowly they went on for what seemed hours. It was hard work for them to go through the lush. It was as tough and fibrous as dried coconut husks. Had it not been for their heavy clothing they would have been cut to shreds in no time. Their hands suffered from the ordeal, but it could not be helped. They had not prepared for such conditions and it was too late to go back. They were at last on the trail of the phantom killer. Only death or inconceivable terror could drive them from it. The man must be apprehended at any cost and each had secretly resolved to see the thing through to a finish. Yet they derived a certain sense of pride from the fact that they were among the first humans ever to tread this strange, blue-tinted world. Police history would long remember them for their daring.

Suddenly there was a violent commotion in the lush not far ahead. Abruptly the intrepid man-hunters halted in their tracks. Machine guns were snapped forward. Then a terrifying shriek rent the stillness. Mortenson's blood chilled and he crouched instinctively. The others did likewise from natural instinct, weapons aimed straight ahead to sweep the wall of vegetation with a deadly fire.

For a moment thereafter the place was as silent as a tomb. Then another shriek came from ahead. Tensely the men waited and then the thing appeared, head and shoulders above the swaying, rolling sea of lush. Barton let out a feverish yell and snapped up his gun. It rattled with a staccato snap. The men stood erect to see an incredible monstrosity staring at them through a triangle of eyes that seemed to spit blue flame.

fortable, for it seemed to bite into them like acid at first. Gradually, as the strange world became clearly defined, they grew accustomed to the force of the violet disk and after a few moments it had risen above the horizon. They had entered the Fifth Dimension at sun rise! On their own world it was well past noon.

Tensed almost to the snapping point, each of the ten men stared about them in search of the horrible creatures Mortenson had told Steckel existed there. Suddenly they discovered that they were actually standing in swaying lush that reached to their shoulders. This came upon them as their eyes began to observe their immediate vicinity. The sudden change of environment had caused them a mild far-sightedness, but now they could see clearly on every side. The lush rolled and swayed like a sea of earthly wheat-stalks in a light breeze.

Mortenson realized in a moment that they would have to mark the spot or their inevitable wanderings would cause them to become hopelessly lost. He yanked his kerchief from a pocket and tied it like a flag to a tuft of the taller plants. It waved feebly in a cool breeze. He turned to Chief Steckel.

"I think it best that we string out in a line, Steckel," he said, his voice sounding microscopically low. "We ought to come upon the phantom bandit's trail in this vicinity. But be careful! He must be desperate and will shoot on sight."

Steckel gave his curt orders. The officers stretched out in a long line. The chief and Mortenson went forward side-by-side with Barton and Riley flanking them. The line swung gradually in a circle around the scientist's hand-kerchief which acted as a centre. The lush seemed un-broken, being so closely grown together that even a small animal would have left visible indications of its passing through it. They continued onward until suddenly the officers at the far end of the line emitted a triumphant yell. Immediately the others surrounded him to find the lush broken in a narrow path through which the desperado had gone. Feet had trampled down one spot. The trail led away from it. The trampled lush in the one place gave them the impression that the man had popped up out of the yielding soil to go marching away.

Barton suddenly stooped over to pick up an object. He handed it to Chief Steckel. It was a black-tipped match-stick.

"We're on his trail, chief," he said excitedly. "He lit a smoke here and tossed the match at his feet!"

Steckel gave a sibilant whistle. "Damned if we haven't traced the snake to his hole!" he snapped. "I hadn't much stock in this scheme, but it looks like his trail, all right. Let's follow it, strung out. He might be hiding in the grass and a line will bring him out."

He started forward rapidly, eagerly. Mortenson grasped his arm.

"Not so fast, Steckel," he warned ominously. "We're not in our own world, but in one unknown. This tall lush might harbor anything. I have no stomach for run-ning into a wandering band of Fifth Dimensional beings."

Steckel fell back instantly. With Mortenson beside him he followed the trail, the others strung out on either side.

The monster of the Fifth Dimension was like an awful nightmare. It had a long, reptilian neck, at the end of which was a venomous-looking head. Its eyes, as large as saucers, were deep set in the forehead, like the three corners of a triangle. From its neck spurted streams of greenish-blue liquid, spilling through the wounds made by Barton's missiles. The enormous head was studded with unnumbered horns and waved back and forth, a long, purple tongue darting from between fang-filled jaws. With a sudden lunge the beast moved toward the men.

"Shoot!" Steckel bellowed, aghast. "Don't stand there like a squad of statues! Shoot!"

The machine guns went into action with an ominous deadliness. The first barrage literally clipped the monster's head from its body. The beast leaped high in the air and fell with a thud, to writhe in the throes of agony and death. Its long, reptilian tail lashed out, beating madly. Finally the creature lay still and the men went cautiously toward it.

The beast had the legs of a centipede, but thick and powerful. The feet were four-toed and savagely clawed. Mortenson was astounded to find a cross between the reptile and the insect and he promptly named it a *serpenta insecteana*.

With a shudder he turned away. The grim-faced man-hunters continued to follow the trail, wondering silently how the phantom bandit had managed to escape the terrifying beast. But the man had had at least a half-hour start on them and Mortenson concluded that the creature had just happened along.

Mile after mile they plodded on, gripping their guns. The phantom bandit, it seemed, had covered mileage at a rapid rate. Finally they entered into a large clearing at the edge of a spectral forest. Weird trees with thick, leafless branches stood before them, but in the clearing they found traces of a fire. The coals were dead and cold.

"The bandit must have stopped here several days ago," said Mortenson to Steckel. "I think he went on into the forest this day. Let's look for the trail at the edge of the trees."

They discovered the trail quickly. It continued onward through an aisle of trees. They followed it single-file now, for the growths were too thick to be penetrated on the sides. The path seemed to be well-beaten but almost every step of the fleeing desperado was marked by the outline of his heels in the yielding soil.

There were other tracks too, that interested Mortenson, causing him considerable apprehension. The foot-marks of the Fifth Dimension dwellers were clearly defined on the trail. The marks were broad, disclosing the outlines of feet that were like those of a monster goose.

Eventually they emerged from the forest. It proved to be merely a mile-wide belt of trees. Now they found themselves in the tall lush again. The trail continued through it. The lush was well-trampled now as though a large party of men had gone through.

After another hour of steady walking, they encountered a series of trails branching from the main path. They paused, baffled.

Looks like we're getting near some town or encampment, Mortenson," Steckel suggested. "Do you think the desperado could have gone on ahead to mingle with the creatures you say exist here?"

"That," said the scientist blankly, "I cannot answer. It is hard to believe, however, that any human could stand on friendly terms with such savage, such grotesque beings. The ones I beheld were indeed savage, though my imagination might have made them more so than they are."

Steckel spat at a large, gargantuan beetle that ambled across the trail. "Which one of these trails do you think we ought to follow?" he asked bluntly.

"I'd follow the center one," said Mortenson, studying the trail closely. "Look! There's a heel print."

VI

Trapped

DOGGEDLY THEY WENT ON. Here and there the man's foot-prints showed clearly, but the others were likewise defined. Mortenson wondered if the band had been finally captured, and was being taken now to some Fifth Dimension village. But his thoughts were diverted suddenly, when the men before him halted. They had come upon another clearing, one that sloped down the side of a rolling hill. Well-worn paths criss-crossed it and in the center stood a squalid town with prim-itive shacks, closely packed together. Off to the left browsed a score or more of strange beasts. Mortenson squinted at them. They were of the same species as was the one which their bullets had destroyed back in the sea of lush! As though sensing the strange visitors, the beasts lifted their heads, eyed them for a moment, and then ambled away.

Something suddenly whined past Steckel's face. It was followed by the dull report of a gun. Instinctively they dodged back out of sight. Steckel looked at Mortenson. His face was white and bloodless.

"He's in that town, Mortenson!" he cried. "He's there!"

"Undoubtedly," replied the scientist, gripping his automatic tightly. "He took a pot shot at us. I saw a wisp of smoke from one of the shacks!"

"Then we've got a fight on our hands, chief," said Barton grimly. "And he's got friends. Let's rush . . ."

A bullet clipped a blade of lush beside his face and he flattened himself. Then came another report. Barton lined his machine gun on the town, but Mortenson held his arm.

"Don't waste bullets, Barton," he advised. "Wait until you see something to shoot at; then let 'em have it."

That *something* was soon to appear, for hardly had Mortenson finished giving his warning to Barton than a score of the strange beasts raced from the back of the town and galloped toward them. Running like mammoth centipedes, reptilian heads high, long tails dragging behind them, they came. The men watched, awestruck. Then a yell from Mortenson broke the spell of awe, that had held them motionless.

"Here they come!" he bellowed, snapping up his automatic. "Look on their backs!"

On each beast rode two or more Fifth Dimension dwellers. They held primitive bows in their hands and had quivers of arrows hanging across their backs. They looked almost human, astride the racing beasts, their long, skinny legs dangling, equally thin arms of which there were four to each creature, waving above their grotesque, egg-shaped heads. They were dwarfted by the size of the monstrous mounts which needed no urging. As they neared the astonished man-hunters, they appeared all arms and legs. Their bodies, blue in color, were short and thick, like the fat belly of a great ape. Their eyes protruded from their faces and waved like the feelers of a snail. And they were equally as loathesome.

"Good God, Mortenson!" Steckel groaned. "We're outnumbered fifteen to one!"

The scientist shuddered, his eyes bulging with terror. "We can't lie here and let them run us down!" he mumbled tensely. "Order your men to shoot their mounts! That'll stop them for the present!"

Steckel stood up impulsively. His head and shoulders rose above the lush. His men lay around him, watching the approaching horde through the vegetation. Before he could give an order, something tugged at his sleeve. A dull report followed and a wisp of white smoke floated from the back of one of the running monsters. Steckel sank with a groan, his left arm feeling numb.

"He got me!" he said dismally. "The killer!"

"Hurt bad, Chief?" Barton quizzed, excitedly.

Steckel shook his head. "Creased me, Barton," he replied. Then he yelled at his men. Instantly the lush at the edge of the clearing became a hornet's nest. The machine guns rattled dully. Mortenson's pistol cracked and his target pitched to the ground. A half-dozen beasts reared up, screamed hideously, and rolled over, spilling their riders headlong. The latter dodged behind the prostrate beasts and showered the ambushers with a hail of arrows.

A shaft buried itself in Riley's chest. He emitted a shrill death cry and rolled over, clutching frenziedly at the arrow. Steckel picked up the detective's machine gun and sent death into more of the running beasts. But there was no halting their mad rush. They continued on toward the men in the lush and the creatures on their backs were either tremendously courageous or too stupid to sense their own danger. They stuck to their mounts until they fell. The clearing was littered with dead and dying. Then the last of the beasts went down under a solid barrage of bullets from the machine guns. It was literally torn to pieces. The riders were buried under it as it rolled over on its back.

Mortenson had a glimpse of a human being running back toward the town. Instantly his automatic went up, but Mortenson had never been a marksman. He emptied his gun at the fleeing desperado and groaned as the man vanished from view. He turned quickly to Steckel. The chief was shooting wildly at the dead beasts hoping to down some of the hideous ceatures shielded behind them.

"Steckel!" Mortenson called to attract his attention. The chief looked around, quizzically. "The bandit just ran into a shack to the left," the scientist continued. "I saw him! He didn't have on his Fifth Dimensional apparatus! We've got to get him before he puts it on and vanishes back to our own world! What do you say we rush the town?"

"We'll be killed, Mortenson!" Steckel declared excitedly. "Those devils will run us through with arrows, before we get half-way across the clearing!"

"There are only a few of them left," insisted Mortenson. "We can make it. It's now or never, Steckel."

Steckel eyed him thoughtfully for an instant and then spoke to Barton.

"We're going to rush the town, Bart!" he said. "Call the men together and let's go!"

"Okay, Chief," said the detective. "We got 'em on the run now!"

He yelled to the men. Two of them were sitting on the ground, fumbling with their apparatus. They were wounded. Riley was dead, his face twisted in a grotesque mask of death. As the remaining men stood up, the two wounded officers vanished as they transferred themselves back to their own world.

With Steckel and Mortenson in the lead, they started across the clearing. A hail of arrows caused them to crouch.

"Split!" yelled the chief. "Barton, you flank the devils and wipe them out!"

Barton ran off to the right to get in the rear of the creatures, who were hiding behind a dead beast. In a moment his machine gun rattled. The others saw several skinny-legged beings leap into the air. They made no sound as they fell back, dead. The attackers had been wiped out, leaving the way clear.

Mortenson, lying on the ground close to a dead dweller of the blue world, appraised the creature quickly. He was a hideous specimen of a strange race. His face was round and his protruding eyes hung limply in death. His mouth was loathesome and was half-open, revealing jagged teeth like those of a deep-sea fish. Around his neck hung a fibre cord to which were attached three silver dollars.

"So that's how the bandit got into the graces of the Fifth Dimension people," he reflected with a nod. "Gave 'em presents same as we do in Africa or Borneo to win respect from the natives."

Steckel's voice suddenly drew his attention. The chief stood erect, gripping his gun tightly.

"Let's go, boys," he said quickly. "The place is clear now and we've got to get that killer!" He turned to Mortenson. "Which shack did he enter, Mortenson?"

"The big one at the left," replied the scientist.

"All right," said the chief. "Now let's spread out and surround it."

The violet sun was standing well west of its zenith. It seemed to cast grim, malignant shadows over the realm of mystery, death and terror. As they went quickly, but cautiously, toward the town, Mortenson felt something sinister in the terrible silence of the place. Surely they had not wiped out its citizens, leaving the phantom bandit there alone to reckon with fate. He decided that this was the case; that the town was merely an outpost, meagerly popu- lated by roving bands of Fifth Dimsension warriors. Per-

haps, too, it was the headquarters of the vanishing bandit!
He wondered if it was.

Then Steckel caught his eye and motioned to him. Instantly the chief broke into a run, closing in on the shack.
It stood somewhat isolated by a narrow, crooked street.
Mortenson followed him and they gained the shelter of
the wall. Strangely, no sound came from the shack. It
seemed as deserted as the town itself. The other men
surrounded it completely, but Steckel and Mortenson were
nearest to its single door.

Cautiously they peered in. It was a place of gloomy
shadows, but on the far side Mortenson caught a glimpse
of a shimmering curtain of blue. He knew what it was
instantly. The phantom bandit was transferring himself
back to their own world, leaving them without further re-
sistance.

With a bound the scientist was in the shack. His pistol
spat twice into the blue haze. He turned to Steckel.

"He's going back to our world, Chief!" he cried. "Call
your men and we'll follow him!"

While Steckel bellowed to his men, Mortenson glanced
around the shack. On the hard-packed floor lay piles of
silver coin. Empty bags littered the floor in one corner.
Stacks of currency of all denominations were piled neatly
to one side. The phantom bandit had certainly made use
of his ability to strike and vanish. Untold wealth lay on
every hand in the unclean hut, but it would have to remain there for the present. He withdrew his fascinated
eyes from it, as the men filed into the room.

"The crook has just returned to our world, men," Mortenson informed them crisply. "We're right on his trail! Press the first two panel buttons together; then press the third. We'll find ourselves within arm's reach of the killer. Be ready to shoot him on sight! Ready? Here we go!"

Instantly the shack glowed with the peculiar pale blue luminosity cast off by the electronic apparatus. As one the men vanished, wondering where they would next appear. Within five seconds vague shapes began to dance before them. Then out of the jumbled maze of dancing, tottering forms they beheld familiar buildings. The dull rumble of traffic reached their ears above the drone of the apparatus. They emerged from the Fifth Dimension to find themselves standing directly in the middle of an intersection. The traffic was at a standstill while the corner signals changed.

Instantly the crowds scattered. Women screamed and fainted. The traffic cop went into action, sensing something was about to happen, and held up the traffic. The bandit's pistol cracked. Mortenson felt a stab of pain in his right shoulder. He dropped his automatic and sagged to the street, a black nausea swept over him. He felt himself dropping into a yawning hole as a machine gun rattled almost in his face. Dimly he saw Barton standing over him, his machine gun spitting flame and death.

For an instant the nausea left him, but the pain in his shoulder increased. Dazedly he looked around. A man was sagging limply near the curb. He was covered with blood and seemed dead on his feet. Then Mortenson recognized the phantom bandit as the man slumped from the curb and fell face-forward into the street. The pain in his shoulder intensified. He fainted.

When he regained consciousness, Chief Steckel and Police Surgeon Wagner were standing beside his cot in the receiving hospital. After a moment he spoke:

"Did you get his corpse, Wagner?" he inquired weakly, his brain still foggy from an anesthetic.

Wagner grinned. "Dead men are sent to the morgue next door, Mortenson," he said. "They've kept a slab ready for the Phantom Bandit. . . ."

"But is he making use of it?" Mortenson cut in anxiously.

"Hell, yes!" replied Wagner. "He's been sleeping on it for two hours! Now be quiet. Sleep if you can. You're not badly hurt, except for a perforated shoulder-blade."

Mortenson felt relieved for the first time in weeks, and promptly went to sleep.

The Red Dimension

A PARTY OF RUSSIAN ENGI-NEERS surveying a desolate part of Siberia came one day upon the body of a man. He had evidently been dead for quite some time and, from the wasted face and limbs, it was concluded he had died from starvation. He carried in his pocket among other things a small pouch in which were found some dirty sheafs of paper on which was scrawled what follows. The thing had little interest for the surveyors and it was my good fortune in being an in-vited member of the party that gave me possession of the

The Red Dimension

papers. Subsequently, I tried to verify the statements made in the manuscript and failed. Though I hunted through countless volumes of the records of Russian courts, I ran across no mention of a Doctor Ivan Korsakoff, or the trial of Arnoldi Kherkoff. Whether this story was only the raving of the poor wretch who was found dead, or whether it had a basis in fact far beyond my ability to discover, I cannot say. I must present the manuscript intact as I translated it, and leave it to my readers to judge.

How I hope to succeed in getting the following narrative to the world is a secret which I never will reveal. Should the channels through which it may reach you be disclosed, then the hands of my jailers would forever seal the lips of those who aided me in giving to the world the true facts of the strange case of my life-long friend and benefactor, Dr. Ivan Korsakoff.

Few people will remember the case. It was given some prominence at the time that the events occurred; but the details were soon forgotten in the frenzied excitement of war and the dethroning of the Romanoffs.

In brief, let me say that I was convicted on circumstantial evidence of having done away with the famous scientist. The evidence I brought in my favor had no effect and I was forthwith sentenced to life imprisonment in a pest-hole in Siberia.

For years I lived in the hope that the truth of Dr. Korsakoff's case might become known. But the passing of years have made me an old man—although I'm only forty—and have caused me to wish that I had received a death penalty. For life has been unbearable! Even now, I lie in a bed of filth praying a humane hand to relieve me of the burden of life.

Perhaps you will be inclined to doubt me when I say I am still confined in a filthy prison camp. You probably believe that such confinement for criminals has been abandoned by every civilized nation in the world. Let me destroy that belief.

In the wastes of Siberia, forgotten by the world, I am destined to remain for the rest of my natural life! Siberian prison camps were the pets of Russian monarchy in the early days. Mine was the most accursed of all, being visited only on rare occassions to receive prisoners and scant supplies. If civilization has actually abolished these places of lingering death, then mine must have been overlooked and forgotten when the Romanoffs met their fate and the monarchy was overthrown!

But the place still exists. Where, I do not know—nor does any other of my pestilence-stricken fellow prisoners.

It is not my intention to dwell too long on the horrible details of confinement here. My main object before I answer the Hand that beckons is to give the world the fact regarding dear Dr. Korsakoff. But first let me tell you who I am. My name is Arnoldi Kherkoff, and I, until my arrest, had hoped to become a great scientist. When I was but four years old, my parents disappeared strangely.

I was left alone—deserted. It was then that Dr. Korsakoff found me wandering aimlessly through the snow-clad streets of Moscow, ravenous, terrified and frost-bitten. He took me at once to his home.

I became his ward and lived with him until the end. He showered me with everything that wealth could offer.

As I grew older, I in turn helped him in his laboratory and learned much about optics and other branches of physics and obtained an inkling of the dimensions beyond ours.

Dr. Korsakoff began to discuss his various experiments with me when I reached eighteen. I was delighted, because it was a sign that I was progressing in the sciences. He could converse with me and receive intelligent replies; and he trusted me not to disclose the nature of his experiments to others.

One day Dr. Korsakoff approached me and laid an affectionate hand upon my shoulder. I looked up from a book I was reading. His face was aglow with excitement and his hand trembled. I surveyed him with alarm, for I felt that excessive work was beginning to affect him. He glanced at the book which now lay on my lap.

"I am pleased to see you reading the treatises in that book, Arnoldi," he said beaming. "How far have you gone?"

"I've reached the chapters that explain Dr. Valenev's magic goggles, sir," I replied, regarding him curiously. "The second chapter tells how he managed to see into an alien dimension. Quite interesting reading matter, sir, but rather fantastic. It sounds impossible."

His hands became still and apparently nerveless. Then his strong fingers sank into the flesh covering my shoulder blade. He seemed tense.

"It is somewhat fantastic, Arnoldi," he said slowly, "but not as impossible as one might think."

"What, sir?" I asked, interested. "Those magic spectacles not impossible?"

"Quite so, my son. It is not at all impossible to see into other planes of life through er-er magic glasses."

"I've never heard of anyone ever doing it except in this book, sir," I protested. "And the experiences set down here sound more like fiction than actual fact. Who was this Dr. Valenev, anyhow?"

"Valenev?" Dr. Korsakoff said, brows arching. "Have I neglected to recount his life to you?"

"Rather I have neglected reading his works, sir," I replied.

"Vladimir Valenev, Arnoldi, was one of the very first Russians to take up the practice and study of optometry in the early days. He was actually the father of the profession in Russia. But his startling discoveries branded him as a fool and he was discredited by the church and state. He was eventually strung up by the thumbs in old St. Petersburg for an exhibition to black magic.

"Most of his statements were without concrete foundation, and they led him presently to his death. Yet for all that, Arnoldi, have you ever thought it might be possible to create a pair of spectacles through which one could see into the beyond?"

I stiffened in the chair and the heavy book thumped on the floor. I surveyed his serious features for a sign that he was jesting.

"I've never thought of such a thing, sir," I said, shaking my head. "In fact I do think it is quite impossible with any glass or series of glasses which we have today."

"Naturally, Arnoldi," he said, "it could not be done with our present chromatic glasses. Yet it is possible to penetrate the beyond—the planes of existence beyond our own."

"What do you mean, sir?" I asked.

"You already know that we exist in a world that wise scientists realize is very limited. Atomic vibration, my dear Arnoldi, has created a varied series of planes of existence, to which the human retina and the human auditory organs are totally out of accord. That is—everything vibrating within the perceptions of our own immediate powers of sense manifests itself in the form of concrete material matter, such as myself and yourself and objects in this room, perceptible by sound, sight, smell, touch, and so forth. Everything below or extremely above our accustomed vibratory limits is to us non existent. You are aware that there are sounds so high in pitch or frequency that the human auditory system cannot hear them. Also there are objects that emit vibrations whose low frequency makes them invisible to the eye."

"You have taught me to understand that, sir," I replied, beginning to have a dim, awed feeling of what was to come.

Surely he had not evolved a pair of glasses adjusting our senses to vibration frequencies beyond our natural limit, for he would have told me of it. But I had learned to know two sides of Dr. Korsakoff. Although he took great pride in explaining his experiments to me, he secretly guarded his plans and formulae until he could offer concrete proof of their feasibility.

"I have tried to teach you much, Arnoldi," he said, "but a complete knowledge of the science of infinite dimensions is too broad for one man. Our span of life is too short—

pliable metal. The backs of them were not unlike the ancient Roman helmets in so far as they extended down to the shoulders where the metal would fit snugly.

The auditory appliance was shaped exactly like the human ear. In the center were small, bright-metal discs which fitted directly into the inner lobe for unhampered transmutation of whatever sounds might come through the magnetic discs from the invisible worlds!

"You see, Arnoldi," the doctor said in explanation, "there are several crystals in each of the sense-transmitting cylinders. Each one was ground with seventy-seven outer facets and double internally. I have cut three different stones and pieced them together in slices to give them the power to transmit the super-sense vibrations. Between each of the lenses, yet below the direct line of vision, are very tiny, high-frequency electrical bulbs. By special transformer I shall lift the voltage through the crystals from a hundred and ten volts to twenty-two thousand. The current will pass finally through the helmets and into the cylinders, creating a transformation of vibrations to our own perceptive limits. The senses of this world are directed to us by a ray, commonly known as the infra-red ray. In a small transparent container behind each of the crystals is an accumulation of *dionium,* a creation of my own. Beyond that, my dear Arnoldi, I can tell you no more about these instruments; for I have constructed them in such a way that caused me to depart from many accepted principles of optics."

He lifted a helmet and fitted it over my head, the cylinders directly in front of my eyes and the auditory systems the powers of apprehension too limited. Yet I mean just what I say about the planes of vision and hearing. I will go even further. I believe there are living material things on these other planes. It will surprise you, no doubt, to learn that I have created a medium through which we may see and hear them!"

I stared at him astounded—fascinated. He smiled down at me with supreme assurance, but without the arrogance that usually accompanies such statements of scientific power. Yet the conception of such a thing was too stupendous for me to grasp all at once.

At the moment I could relieve my tension in no way but to laugh. My mirth seemed to sober him and his features clouded. I felt suddenly ill at ease under his steady eyes and became more serious.

"I'm sorry, sir," I said, grasping his sleeve. "I couldn't help but laugh at the conception. But I simply can't grasp the feasibility of such a thing. It sounds too much like Valenev."

"Arnoldi," he replied impressively, "as we see it the world has been fairly well explored. Yet, if we were to delve into the hidden worlds around us, think of the strange objects and beings that might be seen. Why, the value of the knowledge that could be gleaned from such an adventure would be beyond calculation!"

My head spun at the thought and I stood erect, eager with anticipation.

"You almost convince me, sir," I said, "that such a thing can be done—that such worlds do actually exist."

"It *can* be done, Arnoldi," he replied, smiling again:

"And other worlds *do* exist within our own world! It is possible that we can visit at least several of them. Would you like to see them, my son?"

Trembling I nodded assent. Dr. Korsakoff grasped my shaking hand and wrung it in a firm grip. He placed an arm around me and together we strode slowly toward the laboratory.

As we entered the work-shop which contained practically every known instrument of optical science, and many others, including high-speed lathes, grinding apparatus, measuring devices for facet shaping, and priceless stores of transparent gem-stones, I had a vague feeling that the experiment would see the advent of something unknown to man. I cast a glance at the scientist. His face was stern and serious, although his eyes glowed with excitement. But, could I have realized then what the experiment was to lead to!

He motioned me to be seated before a long quartz-topped table. It shone like myriads of diamonds under the glare of a hanging lamp emitting a strange purplish light. In the center of the table lay two oddly-shaped helmets. From what I believed to be the front of them, there struck out two sets of tapering metallic cylinders. On the sides were accoutrements which I learned were to fit tightly over the ears. Wires ran down from the helmets toward the edge of the table and disappeared beneath it. I surveyed them curiously as Dr. Korsakoff sat down beside me. He picked them up and held one close to me for observation.

Inside the cylinders I saw what appeared to be crystals with hundreds of facets which glittered weirdly under the light. The helmets were oddly designed and of light, snug in my ears. I sat deathly still and closed my eyes while he made certain adjustments, expecting momentarily to find myself looking into a strange world of the beyond. But nothing met my vision. Only darkness—deep darkness.

"Do not be alarmed, Arnoldi." He patted me assuringly. "There is nothing to fear. Just sit still until I adjust my own helmet to the Sixth Dimension, and we will be ready for the experiment."

Presently I heard the hum of a high-speed motor somewhere under the table. It throbbed softly through the auditory apparatus on the helmets. I shuddered at the terrific vibratory movements of the world I began to perceive. Suspended between two worlds, these new sounds grated like steel on my ears. I remembered that such vibrations were alien to the human organs and settled back to wait.

I was startled by a sudden word from Dr. Korsakoff, for it pulled me back to our own world.

"I didn't mean to frighten you, Arnoldi," he said, chuckling. "There's really nothing to alarmed about. I merely wanted to tell you not to jump when I start the current flowing through the helmet. It will sound very weird on your ear-drums. Sit perfectly still and keep your eyes closed for best results. Open them very slowly, and a new world will be revealed. Now be perfectly still, my son. I am switching on the current. You keep your hands on the table. I will control the vibration from a panel at my side. Have an enjoyable visit into the Sixth Dimension— the Red World, Arnoldi!"

I sat with closed eyes for a long time and felt drifting

off. Then slowly I opened my eyes and was stunned by
an amazing brilliancy of vari-hued lights. For a moment
a pain shot through my eyes—they pained to the depths.
Gradually it wore off. Crystals that ranged in color from
deep, unfathomable red to emerald green danced before
me. As though fighting for some control of a color-world
the reds began to seep through into the blues and the
greens.

They suddenly merged into one solid color—the deep,
unfathomable infra-red of the spectrum. The suddenness
of the change caused my whole system to react in a terrific
shudder. Remembering the scientist's words, I clenched my
teeth for control over myself. Now I leaned forward
tensely. Objects were slowly shaping themselves from the
masses. It was the Red World! I thought I was gazing
on a world of fire. Everything shimmered in what appeared
to be a terrific heat. Then, as objects assumed definite form,
I was able to detect the outlines of strange, luxurious vege-
table growths. Weird trees and ferns stood on all sides.

The sky overhead was of a red not less deep than the
more concrete materials of Red Dimension. The earth—
as it appeared, showed in open areas like blood-covered
sandstone. Across it raced what appeared to be heat waves
dancing on a hot, searing surface. Slowly the scene moved.

Then I beheld a rather large clearing completely surrounded by the thick, tangled vegetation. I thought I
caught a slight movement in a patch of swaying lush herbage. I watched the spot tensely.

Slowly, very slowly, the blades parted and out of them
protruded a weird snout. The thing was coming into
view, slinking forward like a stalking panther.

Its nose, like the magnified beak of some grotesque earth-ly insect, pointed to needle thinness, and was pikelike at the base where it protruded from a terror-invoking face! The eyes were like the orbs of an owl, opening and closing with even, rhythmic precision. The creature seemed to crouch ready to spring upon a victim. I wondered at whom or what that death-dealing pike of a snout was aimed. And what did the victim look like? And what were the dimensions of the strange beast or insect of prey? I was soon to learn.

Suddenly the crouching thing hurled itself forward at terrific speed. As it raced on long, slender legs toward the center of the clearing, it appeared in full view to be really an insect. It had three pairs of well-balanced legs that held the segmented body well above the herbage when erect.

Two pairs of wings were distinctly discernible; although they were as transparent as the wings of a dragon fly. They struck outward, apparently to lend speed to the racing thing as it fairly flew across the open. Accompanying its motion there was a dull whir that sounded weirdly in the heavy silence of the red jungle.

I felt as though I were in the jungle, and the thing was coming toward me. I tried to move, even to scream but it were is if I had turned to stone. A frenzy of fright filled me.

But then I perceived another creature even more loath-some than the insect. I tried to close my eyes from it, but a horrible fascination of fright forced me to look at it. It stood, half-crouched, as though waiting for the arrival of a deadly enemy to give mortal combat. Its eyes, protruding from an egg-shaped brow, were concentrated on the coming insect.

As though suddenly sensing that it was being watched by an unseen enemy, it turned its head in my direction for a glance at its invisible audience. The thing's eyes bored into mine for an instant and I suddenly felt very weak and limp.

Probably eight feet tall it stood. From its vile mouth blood-hued saliva dribbled. Loathing filled me. It had four skinny legs that seemed like stilts, jointed well up toward its narrow, straight hips. The abdomen bulged like the belly of some huge boiling pot, and heaved tremulously with each enormous intake or outlet of breath that must have been as foul as the creature itself.

At the end of each leg was a wide, web-shaped foot that covered an enormous area even for so large a monster. Broad-shouldered, with three tentaclelike arms attached to each side, the terrifying creature of the Sixth Dimension stood ready to meet its antagonist.

The arms writhed like so many snakes held together by the heads, their bodies swinging free. The arms on the right clutched at a long spearlike object that appeared to be shaped like a small fan at one end.

Sight of the object, which I accepted at once as being a kind of a weapon, gave me the feeling that this horrible beast was of greater intelligence than the other. Seeing the weapon brought into play strengthened my belief that here was really a creature far above the merely animal, despite its indescribable loathsomeness!

That it was deadly, more deadly than any weapon we on this plane ever possessed, I was soon to learn!

In comparison with the intended victim who now stood with weapon upraised, fanshaped end pointing toward it, the monstrous insect seemed slightly more than half his size.

Yet the insect came on without hesitation, its needle-tipped, natural weapon, aimed at the towering creature. Should the insect actually succeed in reaching the more intelligent creature of the Red World, its pike would doubtlessly run him through from pot-bellied abdomen to the small of the back.

With a sudden roar that echoed and re-echoed in my ears, the larger creature crouched down. Then I heard a whining hiss and from the fanlike end of his spear-shaped weapon shot a sudden beam of strangely mixed reds and yellows.

The ray seemed to begin in a point and widen abruptly as it left the weapon, taking in an area that I had no way of calculating.

At any rate, the racing insect seemed to stop in its tracks and wilt to earth where it lay, trembling violently. Finally it became still.

Then, all at once, the air was filled with a terrible hooting and screeching that chilled my blood. The victor of the uneven battle stiffened at the first outbreak of the violent sounds and swung his protruding eyes around the clearing.

His legs went rigid as though prepared to run, when he beheld a slowly-advancing army of the monstrous insects ringed around the edge of the clearing and treading the low lush herbage with slow deliberate steps as they crept upon him.

As they came on, marching with ominous steadiness, I wondered if any of the upright creature's fellows were near. Surely he had not wandered into this remote section of his world alone.

Immovable as I was I could not look about, and I dared not move for fear that they could see me. But the creature himself seemed prepared for the onslaught. He assumed his crouching position again and pivoted around in a circle. Suddenly the insects rushed. The whir of their movement and the new intermittent hooting, created a battle din in my ears.

Instantly the peculiar rays shot from his weapon and the ground on one side of him was covered with the stricken insects, twitching spasmodically as they died. He spun around in a quarter circle and cut a clean slice from the ranks of the threatening insects.

As he spun around again, I speculated upon the strange scene. What was this? Was it the re-enactment of a scene such as had gone past in the dim days of our own world?

Were these enormous insects the undeveloped life from which had sprung the intelligence of the Sixth Dimension —the Red World? In all probability it must have been! For after all there was a strange similarity between the two forces. The legs and the bodies.

This then, must have been a dreadful battle between the developed and the undeveloped—like the eternal combat of man against beast—beast against man, for supremacy.

Would intelligence on this weird plane of life, as on our own, ultimately predominate?

With panic striking at my reason I watched the battle. The Red World's "man" swung around again with whip-like motion. His rays cleared a clean path through the threatening ranks again. Only one quarter of the circle remained now and the upright creature opened his vile mouth to voice his cry of victory.

It came in a weird maniacal scream that vibrated and re-echoed over the Red Domain like the cry of a preying jungle beast! The insect horde hooted dismal sounds of defeat, but what remained of them came on nevertheless.

Then again came the defiant answering cry of the up-right creature.

He tested the atmosphere with wide, flexible nostrils. Again he voiced his cry of victory. It was answered by a series of exultant roars coming from somewhere deep in the jungles.

Then the creature made his fatal mistake. Expanded to conceit by the victory within his grasp, he lowered his ray weapon and surveyed the remaining insects with contempt. Whether the presence of his fellows, probably not far in the growth, had bred within him a feeling of security, I do not know. But hardly had he lowered his instrument of destruction than the horde of insects closed in on him with astonishing rapidity.

Bewildered at the suddenness and calmness of the rush, the creature roared in a different note, appealing and terror-stricken, and struggled vainly to bring his weapon into play.

It was useless at such close quarters and he cast it aside to grasp six hooting insects in the steel-like grasp of his writhing arms. He crushed them on the instant and hurled them aside. I heard him gasp, when the needle-pointed pikes of the insects began to puncture him.

I caught sight of ghastly mysterious organs protruding from his bulging belly as an insect shook itself loose. He crashed to the ground. Instantly the insects changed the sound of their voices and the ring of high-pitched hootings drowned his cries of death.

At once they set upon the fallen creature. They gouged and tore into his vitals. He managed to keep up a dismal howl even after his vitals had been ripped from his belly. I saw a dozen insects line themselves along his side.

They plunged the pikelike snouts into him and sucked at the thick red substance that was his blood. One lowly creature took hold of the thick skin near the victim's breast. With a jerk it ripped a long streamer of flesh from the body and gobbled it with smacking relish!

That scene was altogether too much for me to stand. I strained and strained to tear myself away from the stone-like immovability that gripped me. Finally I managed to emit a terrible scream and seemed to faint away.

When I opened my eyes once again, I was still in the Red World. Out of the jungle raced a wedge formation of upright creatures, like the slain, with ray instruments, pointed at the devouring insects. With incredible speed they came into the clearing. Instantly the space was aglow with the red and yellow beams.

The insects clambering over the torn and mangled body of the fallen creature lined themselves to meet this new enemy. With an abrupt rush, as though by some signal they advanced toward the oncoming wedge. But before they could cover any amount of space the fatal rays wilted them in their tracks.

Harsh roars echoed through the growths. The features of the upright creatures were even more hideous with rage and they set upon the dying insects to gorge! One insect just to my right seemed to have been untouched. It rose suddenly and attempted to escape. An upright creature detached himself from the gorging mass and gave chase, bringing into play as he ran, his death-dealing ray instrument.

On they came, directly toward me. As they neared I could almost feel the terrific heat of the creatures' bodies. Ghastly features stood in front of my eyes. It seemed to me that hardly a foot of space separated us! I screamed insanely again. Then I saw the upright being lift his ray-gun. The reddish yellow ray seemed to bite into the depths of my eyes. I heard as from far away a deep-throated groan.

I seemed to be flying through space and suddenly, with a jerk, I found myself seated in the chair of the laboratory. I tore frenziedly at the helmet on my head and managed to take it off. Then a dizziness overcame me and a black void. . . .

At any rate, I lay stunned and senseless for what seemed hours. When I finally regained consciousness I opened my eyes to see Dr. Korsakoff sitting stiff in his chair, his helmet still intact. I reached out and grasped his shoulder and shook him. He was cold, his body rigid.

Terrified, I leaped from my chair and swung him around. Oh, God, that I may never witness such a sight again!

The front portion of his helmet seemed to have been cloven with an axe! The vision cylinders hung in shreds and clotted with dried, cracking blood! The lower half of his face seemed to have been beaten into a mass with a blunt instrument!

I screamed like one insane as I removed his helmet. Across his eyes and frontal arch, his skull was cloven in twain! The rays of the Red World had cut a deep gash through which had drifted the life of my dear friend and benefactor.

How I managed to escape a similar fate I do not know unless from my mad movements to remove the helmet.

What must have happened was that our devices, not insulated against things of which Dr. Korsakoff could have known little or nothing, had acted like copper wires in the distribution of electrical energy. The Sixth Dimension beam, then, must have been carried along with our own to strike at us in our own distant plane.

Why tell of what followed—my apprehension for the crime and my conviction?

Now, dear world of which I am but a miserable outcast, praying for death to relieve me of my suffering, let me close this chapter in my book of life. If any story succeeds in reaching the world, the world itself will know and believe that I, Arnoldi Kherkoff, did not murder my beloved benefactor, Dr. Ivan Korsakoff, as the courts of Russia believed.

His was a murderer far beyond powers of man to apprehend.

I suffer for the deed of a being in the Red Dimension—but not for long! I have little fear of the penalties exacted against prisoners of the camp for communicating with the outside world! When they learn of it, life will have already flown.